BUDDHIST TALES
for
YOUNG and OLD

Volume 5

Stories of the Enlightenment Being
Jātakas 201–250

BUDDHIST TALES
for YOUNG and OLD

Volume 5

Stories of the Enlightenment Being
Jātakas 201–250

Interpreted by
KURUNEGODA PIYATISSA MAHA THERA

Stories Retold by
STEPHAN HILLYER LEVITT

Buddhist Tales for Young and Old

Volume 1: STORIES OF THE ENLIGHTENMENT BEING, Jātakas 1–50.
Interpreted by Kurunegoda Piyatissa Maha Thera. Stories Told by Todd Anderson. Illustrated by Sally Bienemann, Millie Byrum, Mark Gilson. 2nd edition, revised and enlarged by Kurunegoda Piyatissa Maha Thera and Stephan Hillyer Levitt. Parkside Hills, New York: Buddhist Literature Society, Inc., 2013. (1st edition, under the title PRINCE GOODSPEAKER, STORIES 1–50, 1995.)

Volume 2: STORIES OF THE ENLIGHTENMENT BEING, Jātakas 51–100, 514.
Interpreted by Kurunegoda Piyatissa Maha Thera. Stories Told by Todd Anderson. Illustrated by John Patterson. 2nd edition, revised and enlarged by Kurunegoda Piyatissa Maha Thera and Stephan Hillyer Levitt. Parkside Hills, New York: Buddhist Literature Society, Inc., 2013. (1st edition, under the title KING FRUITFUL, STORIES 51–100, 1996. 2nd ptg. of the 1st edition, together with KING SIX TUSKER AND THE QUEEN WHO HATED HIM, CHADDANTA-JATAKA (NO. 514) appended, [2004].)

Volume 3: STORIES OF THE ENLIGHTENMENT BEING, Jātakas 101–150.
Interpreted by Kurunegoda Piyatissa Maha Thera. Stories Retold by Stephan Hillyer Levitt. Parkside Hills, New York: Buddhist Literature Society, Inc., 2007.

Volume 4: STORIES OF THE ENLIGHTENMENT BEING, Jātakas 151–200.
Interpreted by Kurunegoda Piyatissa Maha Thera. Stories Retold by Stephan Hillyer Levitt. Parkside Hills, New York: Buddhist Literature Society, Inc., 2009.

Volume 5: STORIES OF THE ENLIGHTENMENT BEING, Jātakas 201–250.
Interpreted by Kurunegoda Piyatissa Maha Thera. Stories Retold by Stephan Hillyer Levitt. Parkside Hills, New York: Buddhist Literature Society, Inc., 2012.

The Ajantā Caves in the Horseshoe-shaped Gorge of the Vāghur River
in the Sahyādri Hills of Maharashtra [Mahārāṣṭra]

Pariyatti Press
an imprint of
Pariyatti Publishing
www.pariyatti.org

First Pariyatti Edition, 2024
Published with the consent of Buddhist Literature Society, Inc.

ISBN: 978-1-68172-661-8 (Print)
ISBN: 978-1-68172-687-8 (PDF)
ISBN: 978-1-68172-688-5 (ePub)
ISBN: 978-1-68172-689-2 (Mobi)
Library of Congress Control Number: 2024936371

Cover illustration by Sally Bienemann, assisted by Arlene Yellen and cover design by Nalin Ariyarathne.

Foreword

This fifth volume of Jātaka stories is a continuation of the translation of Jātaka tales begun earlier.

In this volume, we have retained the format of the last two volumes.

When points are raised in passing in this volume that have been addressed in the footnotes in the preceding two volumes, however, that information is not repeated here. If there is a technical point that is not explained here, the reader is advised to consult the footnotes of the preceding two volumes.

It was mentioned in the "Forward" to the third volume that an audio version of that volume was being prepared. While a good idea for purpose of presenting these stories to a very young audience, it should be mentioned for those who might have been interested in such an audio version for their children that technical difficulties were run into in the preparation of the CDs, so the preparation of these was never finished. And on this account the preparation of an audio version for volumes 4 and 5 was never undertaken.

We have now finished the first two sections [nipāta-s] of the Jātaka tales, which contain 150 and 100 stories respectively. Before we go on to the third, which contains 50 stories, we plan to go back to the first two volumes and revise them so as to include the framing "stories of the present," which were not included in those volumes, add the "connections" between the "stories of the present" and the "stories of the past," introduce the Pāli names of the various stories, indicate the Pāli names of the various characters, and generally revise the format of the first two volumes so as to bring it more into line with that of the third to fifth volumes.

We would like to thank our publisher, The Corporate Body of the Buddha Educational Foundation, for its meritorious efforts in publishing these volumes and distributing them to all who are interested in them free of charge.

South Asians have always loved stories. In the Jātaka tales, we have many very old stories that were taken over and preserved by Buddhism, and given a Buddhist flavor. Some appear as well in the Hindu *Mahābhārata* and *Rāmāyaṇa*, as well as in the popular vernacular literatures of South Asia. In the Northern Buddhist tradition, such stories appear in the Buddhist Hybrid Sanskrit *Jātakamālā* and *Avadāna* literature. Some traveled to Persia where they were incorporated into the Christian 'Tale of Barlaam and Josaphat,' which text translated first into Arabic and then into European languages, became popular in medieval Europe. These stories have indeed traveled worldwide.

It is hoped that a new English translation of the Pāli Jātaka stories will make these stories even further accessible.

The sources consulted in the preparation of the volume at hand are as follows:

1. *Jātakapāli, with the Sinhala Translation*, by Ven. Madihe Siri Paññasīha Mahā Nāyaka Thera, 3 vols. *Buddha Jayanti Tripiṭaka Series*, vols. 30–32. Colombo: Published under the patronage of Democratic Socialist Republican Government of Sri Lanka, 1983–86. Original Pāli Jātaka stories with the Pāli commentary, in Sinhala script with a modern Sinhala translation.

2. *Bhadantācariya Buddhaghosa Mahā Thera's Commentary to the Jātaka Pāli*, rev. and ed. by Ven. Pandit Widurupola Piyatissa Mahā Nāyaka Thera, 7 vols. *Simon Hewavitarne Bequest*, vols. 20, 24, 32, 36, 37, 39, 41. Colombo: Published by the Trustees, 1926-39. Commentary in Pāli on the Pāli Jātaka stories, based on older sources, attributed to the 5th c. C.E. scholar Buddhaghosa. An earlier edition in Sinhala script of the Pāli text in 1. above.

3. *Pansiyapaṇas Jātaka Pota*, by Virasiṁha Pratirāja. Ed. D. Jinaratana. 1927; 5th ptg. Colombo: Jinalankara Press, 1928 A late 13th – early 14th c. C.E. translation of the Pāli Jātaka stories into Sinhala by a minister of Kings Parākramabāhu II, III, and IV.

4. *Pansiyapaṇas Jātaka Pota*, by Vīrasiṁha Pratirāja. Ed. Vēragoḍa Amaramōli. Colombo: Ratnakara Bookshop, 1961. A different edition of 3. above.

5. *Pansiyapaṇas Jātaka Pot Vahansē*, by H. W. Nimal Prematilake. 1963; Rpt. Bandaragama: H. W. Nimal Prematilaka, 1987. Recent Sinhala summaries of the Pāli Jātaka stories.

6. *The Jātaka, together with Its Commentary, Being Tales of the Anterior Births of Gotama Buddha,* 7 vols. Ed. V. Fausbøll. London: Trübner and Co., 1877-1897. Vol. 7 = Postscriptum by the editor and Index by Dines Andersen. The classic Western edition of the *Jātaka*, together with its commentary. Its text is the generally adopted text of the Pāli Jātaka stories in the West.

7. *The Jātaka, or Stores of the Buddha's Former Births*, 6 vols., index. Ed. E. B. Cowell. 1895-1913; Rpt. London: Pali Text Society, 1981. English translation of the Pāli Jātaka stories done by various hands. Contains the stories of the present, which are from the commentary.

8. *Ummagga Jataka (The Story of the Tunnel)*, translated from the Sinhalese by David Karunaratne. Colombo: M. D. Gunasena and Co., Ltd., 1962. Modern English translation of the *Mahā-Ummagga-Jātaka* [No. 546].

The numbers of the various Jātaka stories in this translation are as in 6. and 7. above.

We hope our readers will find this volume readable, readily understandable, and as interesting as they have the preceding volumes.

Peace and health to all!

Kurunegoda Piyatissa Nayaka Maha Thero
Stephan Hillyer Levitt, Ph.D.
May, 2010

Buddhist Literature Society, Inc.
New York Buddhist Vihara,
214-22 Spencer Avenue,
Parkside Hills, New York 11427-1821, U. S. A.

A Guide to the Pronunciation of Pāli Words and Names

VOWELS

a	as *u* in but	u as *u* in pull	ā as *a* in father
ū	as *u* in rule	i as *i* in pin	e as *ay* in say
ī	as *i* in machine	o as *o* in go	

CONSONANTS AND NASALS

k (guttural) like the English *k* in take or pick. kh as *kh* in lakehouse. g as *g* in pig. gh as *gh* in doghouse. The nasal ṅ is used with k, kh, g, and gh.

c (palatal) similar to *ch* in chalk, but unaspirated. ch as *ch* in chalk or church.

j like the English *g* in page. jh as *j* in joy, but even more aspirated. The nasal ñ as in Spanish Español is used with c, ch, j, and jh.

ṭ a retroflex sound, pronounced with the tongue curled back so that it touches the roof of the mouth. ṭh is the same sound, but aspirated. ḍ and ḍh are the voiced counterparts of these sounds. ṇ is the retroflex nasal. The difference between these sounds and the dentals, without dots, is not important for the general reader.

t (dental) similar to *t* in French or Italian. th as *th* in anthill. d similar to *d* in pod or paid. dh as *dh* in roundhouse. The nasal n is used with t, th, d, and dh.

p (labial) as *p* in English up. ph as *ph* in uphill. b as *b* in rub. bh as *bh* in clubhouse. The nasal m is used with p, ph, b, and bh.

ṁ as *ng* in sing. This is a nasal sound that lacks the closure of the organs required for the other nasal sounds.

SEMIVOWELS

y, r, l, v similar to their English counterparts. ḷ is a retroflex variant of l.

SIBILANT

s as *s* in saint or hiss.

ASPIRATE

h as *h* in hit.

Contents

The Story of a Prison
(Bandhanāgāra-Jātaka)

When the compassionate Buddha was living in Jetavanārāma, this story was told about a certain unmarried man who came to be fettered by a wife.

At that time, the king's officials captured some muggers, thieves, highway robbers, and murderous robbers. When they were brought to the king, he listened to the charges against them, and then punished them. Some of them were punished by being put in prison where they were shackled with their hands bound together behind their backs. And some, with their hands cuffed in front of them and chained to shackles around their legs, were tethered to an iron ball.

One day, a monk from a village in the countryside came to visit the city of Sāvatthi. He saw these people who were in the prison. And when he went to see the Buddha, after paying his respects, he mentioned seeing these people who were in the prison. He said, "Venerable sir, I have seen men in the prison. And I think that they will never again be free to associate with everyday people in normal society. Venerable sir, are there in the world any worse prisons than this?" The Buddha said, addressing the monks, "O monks, what sort of a prison is this! The real prison is the prison of sensual desires. That is the true prison that one finds in this world, that one cannot escape easily. It is very difficult to become free from such a prison of sensual desires, even though there are some noble-minded people who have freed themselves from such bondage."

Then the monks invited the Buddha to disclose this story of a prison:

At one time, when King Brahmadatta was ruling the city of Benares, the Enlightenment Being was born to a poor family of cultivators. When he had grown up, his mother became a widow. He helped his mother with her different tasks by providing both for her physical comfort and her mental encouragement. Among other things, he supplied hot and cold water for her to bathe and for her to drink, and for her other needs. All these duties he fulfilled alone.

The Enlightenment Being's mother thought that since her son was fulfilling all her needs at home alone, she would bring a certain young woman from a nearby village for him to marry. She decided to do this without telling him. And she had them get married.

In the course of time, the Enlightenment Being's mother got sick and died. At the same time, the Enlightenment Being's wife became pregnant. But the Enlightenment Being did not know that she was pregnant. At that time, he said, "Darling, I do not wish to live as a layman. I want to renounce the world and practice asceticism." Then the Enlightenment Being's wife told him, "Dear lord, I am pregnant. Please stay at home until after I have delivered the baby. After that, you can become an ascetic." He agreed.

After the baby was delivered, when it was no longer breast-feeding, he decided to leave. But when he told his wife, she said that she was pregnant again. Then the Enlightenment Being thought, "If I ask her permission to leave and renounce the world, this woman will not let me go. Therefore, I have to leave without telling her."

Thinking so, he left his home in the middle of the night and set out on the road. Village watchmen, seeing him, restrained him. Then the Enlightenment Being said to them, "Officers, I did not go out at this hour for any criminal purposes. I am going to the Himalayan forest to practice asceticism there in the forest." Believing his words, they let him go.

The Enlightenment Being fled from that place. He thought, "If I travel at this hour, I will be seized again at some other place. So, it would be good to stay where I am for the night." Staying at an inn that was nearby, early in the morning he left for the Himalayan forest.

Once in the Himalayan forest, he ordained himself to be an ascetic. And he said joyful words about his having become free from the undesirable bondage of the poisonous fivefold sensual desires from which it is not easy to be released, just as from punishment in a prison. There, he became free from the hard to break bondages of household life, parents, children, wife, and all other of the five sensual bondages.

On obtaining such freedom, he attained a joyful mind.

He then started to meditate in the forest. And he attained the five higher knowledges and eight mental absorptions. Without falling away from them, after his death, he was born in the Brahma world.

Saying this, the omnipresent Buddha ended this story of a prison.

The Buddha said further, "The father of that family at that time was King Suddhodana. The mother was Queen Mahāmāyā. The Enlightenment Being's wife became Queen Yasodharā. And the son became I who am today the Buddha."

At the end of this Dhamma sermon, many attained the stream entrance state of mind, the once-returner state of mind, the non-returner state of mind, and the Arahant [sainthood] state of mind.

The moral: "Once one becomes freed from the prison of everyday life, higher states of mind can be attained."

The Story of a Playful Nature
(Keḷisīla-Jātaka)

W hen the omnipresent one who became the master of compassion was living in Jetavanārāma temple, this story was told about the Venerable dwarf Bhaddiya [The Good One].

This is how it was:

The Venerable Bhaddiya was very pious. He was an eloquent preacher, and his voice was very sweet. He attained the highest Arahant-ship, which entails as its highest achievement the fourfold understandings.[1]

A certain monk named Tissa [Good Doer], when going to see the Buddha, saw Bhaddiya near the temple door just as he was entering. He thought that Bhaddiya was a young novice monk. He asked him, "Where are you going, young monk? Come with me." Saying this, he patted him gently on his head and tugged at his robe. Playing with him in this way, he entered the temple. Then he approached the Buddha, first placing his outer robe and bowl to the side of the chamber out of respect. After talking with the Buddha for a time, he asked, "Bhante, where is the dwarf Arahant Bhaddiya who preaches very sweetly? I would like to see him." The Buddha said, "You saw him at the main door. He was the person with whom you played, pulling at his ear. He was the dwarf Bhaddiya."

Hearing these words, the monk Tissa asked the Buddha, "How, Venerable sir, did a monk who was able to attain such a powerful

---

1   The fourfold understandings [catupaṭisambhidā] are understanding the meanings of all words [attha], understanding philosophy [dhamma], understanding the explanation of all words through grammatical and etymological analysis [nirutti], and the power of comprehension and illumination of the foregoing [paṭibhāna].

achievement, having psychic and meritorious powers, become such a short playful object?"

The omnipresent one said, "Oh monk, it is retribution for one of his own bad deeds that he did in the past, that he has become like this. It is the result of nothing other than his own past actions." Then the monk requested that the omnipresent one tell the story of the past. And the omnipresent one disclosed what had happened in the past:

At one time, when Brahmadatta was ruling Benares, the Enlightenment Being was born as Sakka, the king of divine beings. At that time, the king of Benares spent his time enjoying himself at the expense of old people and old animals. He did not like to see old elephants, old horses, or old bullocks. Seeing them, he would capture them and hurt them. He amused himself by playing with old horses. He would break up old carriages by binding new timber to some of the spokes of their wheels, which then, when the carriages are pulled by the old horses, would break up the carts as the wheels go round, hurting the horses. When he would see old women, he would summon them, then beat their bellies and squeeze at the sagging skin, making them afraid of him. When he would see old men, he would summon them and make them roll around on the ground like acrobats. When he did not see any old people, he would ask his servants where old people lived. When they said, "In such-and-such a home, there are old people," hearing this, he would tell his servants to summon them. And then, for his amusement, he would hurt them. People, seeing their parents being hurt like this, and being distressed by their king's shameful behavior, sent their parents away, out of the kingdom. In that country, no one attained merit from giving care to parents. The king's servants also became playful, and did not do their proper duties. As a result of this, all who died in the country were born in the fourfold hells, and no one in heaven.

Sakka, the king of divine beings, did not see as many newborn deities in heaven as before. He decided to investigate why this was so. Once understanding the situation, he decided to tame the king. He took the form of an old man riding in an old wagon, pulled by two old bullocks. Placing in it two jars of buttermilk, he came to see the king on a certain festival day when the king, mounted on a well caparisoned elephant, was in procession in the decked-out city. Seeing the old wagon, the king asked his servants to move the cart to the side of the road. But they could not see the cart, and said repeatedly, "Your lordship, there is no cart." Sakka, by his power, did not let anyone see his wagon except the king.

In the meantime, many people gathered to witness this argument. When many people had gathered, Sakka, by his divine power, drove his wagon over the king and smashed down on the king's head the two jars of buttermilk. The buttermilk soaked his head and clothes, and smelled very revolting. People began to laugh at the king.

Sakka, seeing that the king was distressed, made the wagon disappear and he took his true form with his thunderbolt [*vajjirāvudha*] in hand. He appeared in the sky and said, "Hey, sinful and unrighteous king! Will you never be old yourself? Will not your body be attacked by old age? Why do you playfully hurt old people? By your doing such unwholesome deeds, everyone in your kingdom who witnesses them is born in hell. They have filled it up. People do not get a chance to care for their parents.[2] If you do not stop this behavior, I will cleave your head into two pieces with my thunderbolt. Do not do such deeds again from now on." Saying this, he threatened the king and expressed the good qualities of parents. He explained the value of helping the elderly and its good results. And then Sakka went away. From that time forward, the king behaved differently, behaving as the king of gods had instructed him.

Buddha said further, "Oh monks, as swans and other birds, as well as elephants, horses, and such other animals with four legs are afraid of a lion, just so, Venerable Bhaddiya [like a lion] is small in physical stature, while his other qualities are very noble."

Saying this, the omnipresent one ended the Jātaka story of *Keḷisīla* [playfulness].

---

2   By taking care of one's parents, people can gain a great deal of merit.

"The king of Benares at that time was this monk, the dwarf Bhaddiya. The king of divine beings was I who am today the fully enlightened one."

The moral: "Misplaced playfulness hurts everyone. One ought to respect one's elders."

The Story of Maintaining Life
[The Story of Protecting Life]
(Khandhavatta-Jātaka, Khandhakavatta-Jātaka, Khandhaparitta-Jātaka)

When the omnipresent one who was the foremost compassionate being was living in the Jetavanārāma temple, this story was told about a certain monk who was bitten by a certain venomous snake.

When the monk was chipping firewood in the temple compound, a certain venomous snake came down from a tree and bit him. The monk lost consciousness, and on account of the snake's venom, he died.

This was discussed by the monks assembled in the evening in the preaching hall. As the monks were talking about this, the omnipresent one came in. He asked, "Oh monks, about what were you talking before I came here?" The monks then related to the Buddha what had happened. The Buddha said, "If he had spread loving kindness [mettā] toward the community of snakes, that would not have happened. In the past, by practicing loving kindness toward snakes, people avoided being bitten by them." Then the monks asked the omnipresent one to relate the story of the past. This is how it was:

At one time, when King Brahmadatta was ruling in the city of Benares, the Enlightenment Being was born in a Brahmin family. Giving up the enjoyments of the five sensual desires, he became an ascetic. Living in the Himalayan forest, he became the teacher of many ascetics.

While these were living in the forest like this, there grew up among them a fear on account of many of them being bitten by venomous snakes and dying. They talked about this among themselves, and the

Enlightenment Being heard about it. He instructed them to practice loving kindness toward the four families of snakes. Saying this, he uttered the first spell [*manta*] mentioned in this Jātaka story.

1.   *Virupakkhehi me mettaṁ,*
     mettaṁ Erāpaṭhehi me.
     Chabbyāputtehi me mettaṁ,
     mettaṁ Kaṇhāgotamakehi ca.

The meaning of this stanza is:

> "Let my loving kindness be on the snake family of Virupakkha.
> Let my loving kindness be on the snake family of Erāpaṭha.
> Let my loving kindness be on the snake family of Chabbyāputta.
> Also let my loving kindness be on the snake family of Kaṇhāgotamaka."

He said, "It is good to spread loving kindness on these four families of snakes. Then there will not be danger from snakes."

Saying this, he stated again how to meditate on loving kindness:

2.   *Apādakehi me mettaṁ,*
     mettaṁ dipādakehi ca.
     Catuppadehi me mettaṁ,
     mettaṁ bahuppadehi me.

In this stanza, there is this meaning:

> "Let my loving kindness be upon the beings that have no feet
>   and long bodies.
> Let my loving kindness be upon beings with two feet,
> human beings and birds.
> Let my loving kindness be upon beings with four feet,
> such as elephants, horses, and so forth.
> Let my loving kindness be upon many footed beings,
> such as scorpions, and so forth."

Explaining loving kindness in this way, he made a request of living beings with the following stanza:

3.   *Mā maṁ apādako hiṁsi,*
      mā maṁ hiṁsi dipādako.
      Mā maṁ catuppado hiṁsi,
      mā maṁ hiṁsi bahuppado.

The meaning of this stanza is this:

> "May I not be hurt by any being with no feet!
> May I not be hurt by any being with two feet!
> May I not be hurt by any being with four feet!
> May I not be hurt by any being with many feet!"

After this, he uttered further a fourth stanza, not mentioning any specific living beings:

4.   *Sabbe sattā sabbe paññā,*
      sabbe bhutā ca kevalā,
      sabbe bhadrāni passantu.
      Mā kañci pāpaṁ āgamā.

The meaning of this stanza is:

> "May all living beings, all creatures,
> all spirits, and all others,
> meet only with good things!
> May nothing bad come upon them as a result of
> unwholesomeness!"

Setting things forth in this way, he then explained the value of the three gems, the Buddha, the Dhamma [doctrine], and the Saṅgha [the community of monks]:

5.   *Appamāṇo buddho,*
      appamāṇo dhammo,
      appamāṇo saṅgho.

This means:

"The gem of the Buddha is limitless.
The value of Dhamma is limitless.
The virtuousness of the Saṅgha is limitless."

Saying this, he stated the limitless quality of the three gems. As these are limitless, he mentioned further a sixth stanza to compare the qualities of all living beings with those of the three gems:

6. *Pamāṇavantāni siriṁsapāni,*
    ahivicchikā satapadi,
    unnānābhī sarabu mūsikā.

This means that lengthy creatures like snakes have no wholesomeness. As they have no unlimited wholesome qualities, they are limited. Explaining it in this way, he mentioned various feared living beings like venomous and venomless snakes, scorpions, centipedes, spiders, lizards, mice, and so on.

He instructed that loving kindness should be practiced toward them as well:

7. *Katā me rakkhā, katā me parittā.*
    Paṭikkamantu bhutāni.
    So 'haṁ namo bhagavato,
    namo sattannaṁ sammā sambuddhānaṁ.

He said this latter stanza to remind everyone of the high qualities of the three gems. It means:

"I am giving protection. I am giving guardianship.
Those who have bad thoughts toward me, please leave.
I am a person who bows down to the virtuous Buddha
who came before, and I bow down to the seven Buddhas,
        who include the Buddha Vipassī."[3]

---

3   The seven Buddhas are Vipassī, Sikhī, Vessabhū, Kakusandha, Konāgamana, Kassapa, and Gotama. These are Buddhas of different world ages, Gotama

In this way, he taught the spell for protecting life [*khandhaparitta*]. From that point on, the ascetics no longer had any danger from snakes.

Saying this, the Buddha ended the Jātaka story of maintaining life [*khandhavatta*].

The Buddha then mentioned that the ascetics at that time were now the followers of the Buddha and he, who is today the Buddha, was at that time their chief advisor.

The moral: "Loving kindness is the most important practice in bringing freedom from fear to the world."

---

being the Buddha of our present age. Gotama's coming is said to have been foretold by Kassapa.

(204)

The Story of Vīraka
(*Vīraka-Jātaka*)

The omnipresent one who realized his omnipresence on his own, while he was living in the Bamboo Grove [Veḷuvanārāma] related this Jātaka story with regard to imitating the omnipresent duties of the Buddha.

When Devadatta had taken 500 monks away from the Buddha's community, the two chief disciples [the Venerable Sāriputta and Moggallāna] then went to those monks and preaching about the virtuosity of the Buddha, they requested them to return to the Buddha's fold. In this way, they brought them back to the Buddha.

When they returned and the omnipresent one saw them, he asked, "When you were coming back with these monks, what was the Venerable Devadatta doing?" The two chief disciples said, "He was trying to imitate the omnipresent one's magnanimity. But even though behaving like that, he was developing a great amount of angry thoughts toward the Buddha."

The Buddha heard these words and said, "The Venerable Devadatta tried to imitate me not only now but also in the past, and thereby he came to ruin."⁴ Hearing this, the community of monks asked the Buddha to disclose the story of the past. And the Buddha told the story in this way:

At one time, when King Brahmadatta was ruling in the city of Benares, the Enlightenment Being was born as a water crow living in a certain pond. He was named Vīraka.

Because of a severe famine at that time, there was a scarcity of food. People did not give food to crows at that time, as if food were itself golden coins.

---

4   This is a common theme regarding Devadatta. Compare, for instance, the *Virocana-Jātaka* [No. 143] and the *Vinīlaka-Jātaka* [No. 160].

A crow called Saviṭṭhaka who was living in Benares at that time went with his wife to the lake where the Enlightenment Being was living, and paid respect to the Enlightenment Being. The Enlightenment Being asked, "Why did you come here?" Saviṭṭhaka said, "Your lordship, I came here to serve you with my wife." The Enlightenment Being agreed to this. From that time on, the crow Saviṭṭhaka was given fish by the water crow, and he ate as much as he wanted until he was satisfied, giving the remainder to his wife. The two of them lived happily there by the lake.

While they were living happily like this, one day Saviṭṭhaka spoke to his wife. He said, "This water crow is black, and he has two feet. I also am black, and I, too, have two feet. Why should I eat prey killed by him? I myself can catch prey, and can eat my own prey." Thinking this, one day he approached the water crow and said, "Friend, I am no longer going to eat the prey caught by you. I will eat what I can catch on my own." Hearing this, the water crow said "One has to dive and swim in the water in order to catch fish. This will not be as easy for you to do as it is for me. You might not be able to do it as I do." But Saviṭṭhaka did not listen. Thinking that he would eat his own catch, he went into the water, but got entangled in some water plants, swallowed water, and died.

Saviṭṭhaka's wife, the she-crow, became worried when Saviṭṭhaka did not return from the lake. She went to the Enlightenment Being and said, "Your lordship, have you seen the crow Saviṭṭhaka who has a sweet voice and a neck with a dark blue sheen like a peacock's neck?" And the water crow called Vīraka said, "Without paying heed to my words and having become conceited, he went down into the water, his feet became entangled in water plants, and he died."

On hearing these words, the she-crow wife cried out, wept uncontrollably, and went back to the city of Benares.

Saying this, the Buddha ended this Jātaka story of Vīraka.

"The conceited crow who died at that time trying to behave like the water crow was Devadatta. The water crow was I myself, the Buddha, the most noble one in the world."

The moral: "Know your own limits before trying to do something."

The Story of One Born in the Ganges River
(Gaṅgeyya-Jātaka)

This Jātaka story was told by the omnipresent one who had tenfold powers [bala-s][5] when he was living in the Jetavanārāma in Sāvatthi about two young monks.

Two young men who lived in the city of Sāvatthi became ordained in the Buddha's dispensation after becoming pleased with the Dhamma [the Buddha's teachings]. They practiced meditation on the loathsomeness of the body. But instead of developing their minds with wisdom, they clung to their attraction to their bodies' beauty and became conceited thinking about how handsome they were. They then fell to arguing as to which one of them was the more handsome. As they could not decide as to which of them was the more handsome one, they went to an old monk and asked, "Venerable sir, which of us is the more handsome?"

The old monk said, "Instead of you looking at one another, look at me! I am the most handsome of the three of us." Then the young monks said, "We asked you one thing, and you answered us something different." Saying this, they got upset and stormed off with anger in their minds.

This event was talked about in the preaching hall by the assembled monks. While they were discussing this, the omnipresent one came in and asked, "Oh monks, what were you discussing before I came here?" The monks told the Buddha about what they were talking. The Buddha said,

---

5   The ten (super-normal) powers of a Tathāgata, or Buddha, consist of his perfect comprehension in ten psychic fields of knowledge. The Buddha is also said to have the physical strength, or power, of ten times that of an elephant of the highest caste of the ten castes of elephants. Each of the ten castes of elephants is said to have ten times the strength of the immediately lower caste.

"Not only in the present, but even in the past these two monks argued over their physical beauty." And the Buddha was asked to tell the former story. The Buddha then disclosed the story of the past. This is how it was:

At one time, King Brahmadatta was ruling the city of Benares. The Enlightenment Being was born then as a tree spirit on the bank of the Ganges River.

At that time, one fish called Gaṅgā met another fish called Yamunā and they began to argue as to which of them was the more beautiful. Arguing like this and not being able to come to a decision, they approached a tortoise that they saw by the bank of the river and asked him, "Which of us is the more beautiful, Gaṅgā or Yamunā?"

The tortoise answered, "The fish called Gaṅgā is very beautiful, and the fish called Yamunā is also very beautiful. But more beautiful than either is a tortoise with a body round like a spreading banyan tree, with a shell, with a head and neck long like the yoke of a chariot, and four-footed."

On hearing these words, the two fish got very angry and said, "We asked you one thing, and you answered us something different. We asked you about our beauty, and you replied about yours." And they moved about angrily fluttering their fins, and splashed water on the tortoise.

Saying this, the Buddha ended this Jātaka story about one born in the Ganges River.

"The two fish at that time were these two young monks. The tree deity who saw this was I who am today the Buddha."

The moral: "Foolish people argue unnecessarily about unimportant things."

The Story of a Deer of the Kuruṅga Species
(*Kuruṅgamiga-Jātaka*)

The Buddha told this story when he was living at the Bamboo Grove temple with regard to Devadatta.

At that time, the Buddha heard that Devadatta was trying to kill him. Hearing the news about the conspiracy, the Buddha said to the monks, "Oh monks, not only today has Devadatta tried to kill me, but also in ancient times he tried to kill me, too." And the Buddha then disclosed the story of the past.

Long ago in Benares, when King Brahmadatta was ruling, the Enlightenment Being was born as a deer of the Kuruṅga species. He lived in a thicket near a certain lake. Near that same lake, there was a huge tree in which there lived a woodpecker [*satapatta*], and in the lake there lived a tortoise. The three became friends.

At that time, one evening, a certain hunter laid a snare made out of the veins of an animal, and he went away. The Enlightenment Being became bound in the trap early in the morning, before dawn. He tried to break the snare, but could not do it. Becoming afraid of death, he began to cry out. Hearing the cries of the deer, the woodpecker and the tortoise came there and saw that their friend was bound in the snare. Thinking that it is a good thing to save one's friend from danger, they approached the snare. The woodpecker said to the tortoise, "Friend tortoise, you have sharp teeth in your mouth. So you can cut through the snare. While you are cutting through it, I will stop the hunter from coming here." Saying this, the tortoise began to gnaw at the snare. And the woodpecker flew to the hunter's hut and sat on its roof.

Before the sun came up the hunter, thinking that it was a good time to go out, took his knife in hand and started to leave the hut. At that moment the woodpecker, crying out with a shrill noise, flew down from the hut's roof and flapped his wings at the hunter's face. The hunter became upset and said, "This inauspicious bird has come into contact with my body." He went back into his home and lay down, waiting for a short while before going out again.[6]

The woodpecker then thought, "No doubt, the hunter will now come out through the back door." Thinking this, he went near the back door and sat there. The hunter, just so, thought this time he would go out the back door. And this time, also, the woodpecker screeched and flapping his wings, hit the hunter on his face. Then the hunter became very upset and said, "This inauspicious bird has come into contact with my body again. This is a very bad omen." Thinking this, he went back inside the hut. "It is not good to go now. I will sleep and get up after sunrise. I will go to hunt when there is daylight." And he slept. When sunrise came, he started to leave. When he left for the third time, after sunrise, the woodpecker flew fast to the lake and told the deer and tortoise that the hunter was coming. By that time, the tortoise had gnawed through two of the three sinews of the snare. His teeth were in pain, he was bleeding from his mouth, and he was lying down and feeling faint.

Then the deer, seeing the hunter in the distance with his knife in hand, jumped fast and broke the last sinew of the snare. He ran into the forest. The woodpecker flew to the top of his tree. But the tortoise did not have enough strength to go anywhere, so he just lay in that spot. The hunter, coming there, as he could not carry the tortoise, put him in a bag and tied it with one of the sinews from the trap to a branch of a tree that was stuck into the ground. This action was seen by the deer who, deciding to save his friend's life, let the hunter see him. The hunter then chased the deer.

---

6   In some parts of South Asia, hearing a woodpecker cry out first thing in the morning is taken to be a bad omen. For such an omen to come into physical contact with you, is even worse.

The deer did not run so fast that the hunter would not be able to catch up to him, but he did not let the hunter catch him. He led him deep into the forest. And when the hunter came near, he ran off into the forest. In this way, he deceived the hunter. The deer doubled back by a shortcut to the lake where the tortoise was, and quickly he tore open with his antlers the bag in which the tortoise had been placed. He said, "Oh tortoise, come out quickly and dive into the water. And woodpecker, go high up into the tree." In this way, he made sure that both of them were safe. And he ran back into the deep forest.

The hunter returned there and did not see the tortoise in the empty bag. Without saying anything, he went home.

The Buddha, in this way, disclosed this story of a deer of the Kuruṅga species.

"The hunter at that time was the monk Devadatta. The woodpecker was the Venerable Sāriputta. The tortoise was the Venerable Moggallāna. And the deer of the Kuruṅga species was I who am today the Buddha."

The moral: "Good friends can help one overcome difficulties."

The Story of Assaka
(Assaka-Jātaka)

Again, on some other occasion, the omnipresent one who became senior to all living beings in the world disclosed this Dhamma story with regard to the former wife of a monk. This is how it was:

One monk, after his ordination, had his mind constantly distracted with thoughts of his previous wife. The Buddha said to him, "Oh monk, you are still infatuated with your former wife. Yet she has no desire to be together with you any longer. Even before this in the ocean of re-becoming [saṁsāra] you have suffered a lot on her account." Saying this with regard to a story of the past, the omnipresent one was then invited by the monks present to disclose the old story. The Buddha then related it in this way:

Long ago, there was a king named Assaka ruling the city of Patali. He had an especially beautiful queen named Ubbarī who was more beautiful than all other women. She was endowed with the five physical beauties, and resembled a divine damsel.

This beautiful chief queen passed away prematurely in the middle of her life because of a certain congenital sickness. As the king was infatuated with her, he became very sad and was inconsolable. He placed her body, embalmed with oil, in a coffin set near where he slept. And he did not eat or drink for seven days. His ministers and other well-intentioned people told him, "Your lordship, all things are impermanent. Therefore, please do not be consumed with grief." Even though they advised him in this way, they could not allay his grief. And he spent seven days without eating or drinking.

At that time, the Enlightenment Being who had fulfilled the tenfold perfections [pāramī-s, later pāramitā-s] had ordained himself an ascetic in the Himalayan Mountains. He attained the fivefold mental absorptions [*jhāna*-s], and passed his time engaged in them. One day, he was viewing the world with his divine eye [*dibbacakkhu*] and he saw King Assaka's suffering. He decided, "I will go and release him from his suffering." Thinking this, he went by air to Patali and alighted in the royal garden, sitting under the Sal tree [in the center of the garden] like a golden image. Then, there came a certain young Brahmin and the ascetic asked him, "Oh young man, is your king a righteous man? Does he rule your country according to the tenfold rules of righteous kingship [*dasarājadhamma*]?" The Brahmin youth said, "Your worship, he does so. But unfortunately his head queen has recently passed away. Because of that, the king laments and weeps inconsolably. Your worship, the king needs consoling by someone like you. If possible, please visit our king and comfort him." Then the ascetic said, "Young man, I do not know the king. If I knew him, I could show him his queen's life in her new re-becoming [*punabbhava*; in popular parlance, rebirth]. And then he would be able to set aside his grief."

Then the young Brahmin, hearing this, said, "Your worship, I will bring the king here. Please wait here until I return with him." Saying this, he left to go to the king, and he told him about the ascetic. The king heard that there had come a certain ascetic with a divine eye, and he thought, "There is no doubt that this ascetic will know my queen's new birth. Therefore, I must go to see him." Thinking this, he went to the royal garden with his ministers. Seeing the ascetic, he asked him, "Your worship, do you know my beloved queen's re-becoming?" The ascetic said, "Yes, your lordship, I know where she has been born anew." The king said, "If so, please tell me." The ascetic said, "She has been born as a dung beetle [*gomayapāṇaka*]."[7] The king said, "How can such a beautiful woman, with such physical beauty, have been born as a dung beetle? How can I believe this?" The ascetic then said, "If that is the case, should I bring her here to show her to you?" The king said, "Yes, sir."

---

7   This beetle lays its eggs in a ball of cow dung. When the young beetles are born, they eat the cow dung and grow large by this.

Then the ascetic commanded by his psychic power that the cow dung beetle and her mate that were busy nearby rolling two balls of cow dung should come before them.

The female dung beetle came following the male dung beetle, each rolling a cow dung ball. The ascetic said, "The second dung beetle who is following the male is your queen Ubbarī." Further, he said, "Your lordship, because your queen was intoxicated with her physical beauty, she failed to do any good or meritorious deeds. So she was born like this." He said, "Should I ask her to speak?" The king said, "Yes, please do!" Then the ascetic addressed Ubbarī, "Oh Ubbarī, can you tell me your former birth and lineage? Do you still love your former husband?"

Then the female dung beetle said, "Your ascetic worship, the king and myself in the past on many occasions enjoyed ourselves very much in this park. Now, separated from my king by re-becoming, what type of emotional attachment can I have to him?" Hearing these words, the king lost his attachment to her. After that, the king had the queen's body removed from the palace, and he washed his head and body. According to the ascetic's advice, he ruled the country righteously. And in the course of time, he passed away.

Saying this, the Buddha ended this Jātaka story of Assaka.

"King Assaka at that time was this lovesick monk. The monk's former wife with whom he is infatuated was Queen Ubbarī. The Brahmin youth who spoke with the ascetic about the king's grief was the Venerable Sāriputta. And the ascetic was I, myself, who has become the Buddha."

The moral: "Everything is impermanent. Even though you may have an enjoyable time with someone, when people move on, they lose their old attachments."

The Story of a Crocodile[8]
[The Story of a Monkey]
(Suṁsumāra-Jātaka, Makkaṭa-Jātaka)

This Jātaka story was disclosed by the omnipresent one when he was at Jetavanārāma on account of an attempt to kill him by Devadatta. This is how it was:

One day, the community of monks was assembled in the preaching hall and was discussing the attempt by Devadatta to kill the Buddha. When the Buddha entered, he asked, "Oh monks, what were you talking about before I came here?" On hearing that they were talking about Devadatta's recent attempt to kill him, he said, "Oh monks, not only today, but even in the past he tried to kill me. But in trying to do so, he could not even generate fear in my mind." The monks then requested that he disclose the past story. The Buddha disclosed the story in this way:

At one time, when King Brahmadatta was ruling the city of Benares, the Enlightenment Being was living as a monkey in a forest near a riverbank. He spent all his time there.

At that time, a pregnant she-crocodile, on seeing the Enlightenment Being who was this monkey, got a craving to eat his heart.[9] She said to her husband, "My master, there is a very strong monkey king on the bank of this river, and I bear a craving to eat his heart." The crocodile husband

---

8   A *suṁsumāra* is a gavial, a large harmless vegetarian crocodile of India (*Gavialis gangeticus*). Compare the Buddhist Sanskrit version of this story in the *Mahāvastu* and also the versified Pāli version in the *Cariyā-Piṭaka*. And compare the story in the *Vānarinda-Jātaka*, Jātaka No. 57 in Vol. 2 above.

9   When pregnant, females are subject to unusual cravings.

said, "My love, we live in the water and are water-dwelling animals. He lives in trees in the woods on dry land. How can I get his heart? I may not be able to do it."

Hearing this, the she-crocodile said, "My loving master, you must get it for me by whatever stratagem you know. Do you understand? If you do not bring it for me, I will die." Hearing her words, the crocodile said, "All right. I will do whatever I can." And he went near the tree where the monkey king lived and said, "Friend monkey king, why do you put up with eating the unpleasant bitter tasting fruit and leaves on this side of the river? When I see the other side of the river, I can see mangoes, rose apples, wood apples, breadfruit, palm trees, and other such sweet-tasting fruit and leaves. It would be better for you to live on the other side than on this side of the river."

On hearing these words, the monkey king replied, "Friend crocodile, the river's water is very deep and wide between the two banks. I cannot jump across it. What else can I do?"

Then the crocodile said, "If you would like to go there, sit on my back. I will take you across the river."

The monkey king then said, "All right. Let me see your back." And the crocodile came near him, showing him his back. The monkey king jumped up on his back. Then the crocodile, taking the monkey king on his back, went into the middle of the river and started to submerge himself in the water. The Enlightenment Being then asked, "What is this, my friend? While taking me, you are letting me drown in the water." Hearing his words, the crocodile said, "Do you think that I am one who would give you sweet fruit? I want to give the meat of your heart to my loving wife by killing you. That is why I am carrying you."

Hearing the words of the crocodile, the monkey king said, "It is good for you to have told me that. Do you think that a monkey keeps his heart in his chest? Jumping here and there, it would be torn into pieces." Then the crocodile said, "If that is so, then where is your heart?" The Enlightenment Being said, showing him a nearby rose apple tree on his side of the river with well ripened fruit hanging on the tree, "Look at that tree. Those hanging red things are monkeys' hearts. My heart is also hanging there."

The crocodile said, "Then I will not kill you, if you promise to give me your heart." Saying this, he took the monkey back to his side of the river. Once there, the monkey king scurried up into the tree and said, "Foolish crocodile, I no longer want your mangoes and rose apples on the other bank of the river. Do you think that monkeys' hearts are on trees? Your body is big, but your sense is little. You did not understand that I was trying to deceive you. Go back to your own place." And he sent him away.

The crocodile became very upset, as if he were a person who had lost 1,000 gold coins gambling. And he went away to the place where he lived.

Saying this, the omnipresent one then ended this story of a crocodile.

"The she-crocodile at that time was the damsel Ciñcā. The monk Devadatta was the crocodile. And the monkey king was I who am today the Buddha."

The moral: "The bad intentions of foolish people can be easily overcome by the wile of noble ones."

The Story of a Kakkara-bird[10]
(Kakkara-Jātaka)

At one time, when the omnipresent one was living at Jetavanārāma, there was a young monk living in Venerable Sāriputta's nearby temple on its grounds. This story was delivered by the Buddha on account of this young monk's fastidious way of living. The circumstances of its delivery are as follows:

One of the Venerable Sāriputta's young disciple monks was very careful with regard to the protection of his body. In order to maintain his health, he did not eat hot rice thinking that if he were to eat it he might upset his bile.[11] So in the hot weather, he did not eat hot rice. In this way, he safeguarded his health.

One day, the monks who were assembled in the evening in the preaching hall to listen to the Buddha's evening Dhamma sermon, having heard about this, were discussing it. As they were talking about it, the omnipresent one entered the preaching hall and asked, "Oh monks, what were you talking about before I came here?" The monks told the Buddha that they were talking about this young monk. The Buddha said, "Oh monks, not only today in his present life does this young monk protect his well-being with care, but also in the past he did so and he thereby saved his life." The monks then asked the Buddha to disclose the past story. And the Buddha disclosed the story hidden by time. This is how it was:

---

10   A Kakkara [Sinh. *koravakā*] is a small aquatic bird that lives near paddy fields and in forests with muddy waters in South and Southeast Asia.

11   By South Asian Ayurvedic medicine, one's health depends on a proper balance of the three humors, air, bile, and phlegm.

At one time, when King Brahmadatta was ruling in Benares, the Enlightenment Being was born in a forest as a tree-deity.[12] At that time, a bird hunter captured a certain female bird and intending to use her as a lure, he planned to capture male birds in his snare placed nearby her. In this way, he used to capture birds.

Once he tried to capture a certain Kakkara-bird that by its luck had formerly freed itself from another bird hunter's snare. Because it had once been caught in such a snare, it knew how to avoid being caught this time. And so the bird hunter could not capture him. On this account, the bird hunter became angry at this bird, and he tried over again and over again to capture him, setting his snare here and there. Days went on, and he could not get him.

Then the bird hunter thought, "If I cannot capture this bird in my present snare, then I will capture him by another stratagem." Thinking so, he disguised himself as a small tree with a cage-like snare placed on one of the branches, and he wandered from here to there in the forest in places where this bird would frequent. The Kakkara-bird, seeing the bird hunter disguised in this way, thought he would let him know that he recognized him. He said, "I have wandered in this forest in many places. I have been in mango trees, rose apple trees, breadfruit trees, wood apple trees, Kitul palm trees. But I have never seen a tree that wanders. I am not deceived by your trickery." Saying this, loudly he made a cry, and he flew away.

The bird hunter understood that he had been recognized by the bird and said to himself, "Oh, this bird recognized me and broke the palace I had built for him in the sky. He knew my thieving intentions to steal his life." Thinking this, he also went away after capturing some other birds that he was able to get.

Saying so, the Buddha ended this story.

---

12   According to Buddhist teachings, living beings who have performed meritorious deeds can be born as either tree-deities or gods in the divine worlds, in accord with their past deeds.

"At that time, the bird hunter was the monk Devadatta. The Kakkara-bird was the fastidious young monk who is very careful with regard to protecting his body. And the tree-deity who witnessed this incident was I who am today the Buddha."

The moral: "One's care for his or her well-being pays off."

$$\boxed{210}$$

The Story of a Woodpecker
Named Kandagalaka
(*Kandagalaka-Jātaka*)

The omnipresent one who became the chieftain of the world delivered this Jātaka story while he was living in the Bamboo Grove temple so as to explain the monk Devadatta's desire to imitate the Buddha. The circumstances of this are:

One day, the monks assembled in the preaching hall in the evening were discussing Devadatta's desire to imitate the Buddha. When the Buddha entered, he asked, "Oh monks, what were you talking about before I came here?" The monks told him about what they were talking, and the Buddha said, "Oh monks, not only today, but even in the past Devadatta fell into deep suffering by trying to imitate my status." Hearing this, the monks invited the Buddha to relate the story of former times. The omnipresent one then disclosed the past incident. This is how it was:

At one time, King Brahmadatta was ruling the kingdom of Benares. At that time, the Enlightenment Being was born as a woodpecker in a forest of turpentine trees with the name Khadiravaniya [One Who Dwells in a Forest of Turpentine Trees]. There he dwelt.

Another woodpecker was born nearby with the name Kandagalaka [Swallower of Worms and Insects in the Stems of Trees]. He lived in a forest with tender timbers, and he became friendly with the woodpecker who was the Enlightenment Being. When he visited the Enlightenment Being, the Enlightenment Being used to offer him the insects that he had gotten from pecking the turpentine trees in his forest. Kandagalaka swallowed them as if they were honey cakes. In the course of time, Kandagalaka thought, "My friend here is a woodpecker, and so am I. I, too, can get food from these turpentine trees just as he does." Thinking so, one day he said to his friend, "My friend, I, too, can peck the same turpentine trees that you peck. Therefore, do not trouble yourself by pecking food for me." The woodpecker who was the Enlightenment Being said, "You are able only to peck at trees with tender timber. You cannot peck hard timbered trees such as turpentine trees." Hearing this, Kandagalaka became overly proud and said, "Why cannot I do just as you do?" And he flew away with speed. Alighting on a turpentine tree, he pecked at it, broke his beak and wounded his head, and his eyes went up in his head. This was very painful to him, and he fell to the ground unconscious. When he regained consciousness, he murmured by reflex, "What is this firm tree with thorny leaves that is like iron?"

The Enlightenment Being said, "Without listening to me, and without the ability to peck hard trees, you now have fallen into hardship. These trees are known as turpentine trees."

And Kandagalaka died in that same spot.

Saying so, the Buddha ended this story of a woodpecker named Kandagalaka.

"At that time, the woodpecker named Kandagalaka was the monk Devadatta. And the woodpecker born with the name Khadiravaniya was I who am today the Buddha who has attained enlightenment."

The moral: "It is always good to know your limits."

The Story of the Brahmin Somadatta
[The Moon-Given One]
(*Somadatta-Jātaka*)

This story was delivered by the omnipresent one who became the leader of the world while he was living at Jetavanārāma in Sāvatthi on account of the Venerable elder Lāḷudāyī [Udāyī the Simple One]. The circumstances of this are:

When the Venerable Lāḷudāyī was in the middle of a group of people he could never express what he wanted to say. He would always say the opposite of what he wanted. One day, the monks gathered in the evening in the preaching hall were discussing how he talked foolishness before the Buddha came there. When the Buddha arrived, he asked, "Oh monks, what were you talking about before I came?" The monks told him what they were talking about and the Buddha said, "Oh monks, not only today, but even in the past Lāḷudāyī was like this." And the monks requested the Buddha to disclose the story of the past. The Buddha then disclosed the past story.

At one time, when King Brahmadatta was ruling the kingdom of Benares, the Enlightenment Being was born in a Brahmin family in Kāsi with the name Somadatta. When he was grown up, he was sent to study in the city of Takkasilā with a well-known teacher. There he excelled in his studies. He thought, "Let me return to my parents as they are poor. Once there, I will be able to serve the king while looking after them." Thinking so, he returned to Benares.[13] After returning, he gained employment in the king's palace. He became very faithful to the king. In the meantime, one of his father's two oxen died. The father said to his son, "My son

---

13   Kāsi was a suburb of Benares at that time.

Somadatta, one of my oxen has died. I now cannot plough my field as I have only one ox left.[14] Can you please help me to get another ox by asking the king for one?"

The Enlightenment Being then said, "My dear father, as I am so close to the king, it would not be proper to take advantage of my position and ask this of him, especially now at this time. You must ask the king on your own, and then he will give you another ox."

The father said, "My son, you must understand that I am unable to speak in the presence of more than one person. If I intend to ask for an ox, I will end up asking him to take the ox I have. This is not a good idea. It will not result in the king's giving me an ox." The son then said, "You must ask the king on your own, whether it results in you getting an ox or giving the king your existing ox. I will teach you what to do." And he fashioned a certain verse:

"I had two oxen to plough my field.
One died. Your lordship, please give me another one."

The son said, "When you see the king, bless the king saying, 'May you live long, your lordship, winning every battle!' Then say this verse:

'I had two oxen to plough my field.
One died. Your lordship, please give me another one.'"

The father said, "Oh my son, I am unable to remember this verse."

So the son told his father to take as long as he needed to learn the verse. And he showed him a quiet and lonely place where he could go to memorize it. There, using clumps of grass set up as the people in the king's assembly, he instructed his father, saying, "This is where the king sits. This is where the chief minister sits." And explaining everything in this way, he removed his fear. And in this way, he countered his father's lack of confidence.

---

14 As the Enlightenment Being's father was so poor and had no other means of livelihood, he engaged in cultivation. Normally, Brahmins shun such occupation.

In due course, the father learned the verse by heart. And he told his son, "Now I can go to the king." The Enlightenment Being then got a suitable gift for his father to give the king, and told his father, "Now you can go see the king."

The son went along with his father to see the king. Seeing the king, the father said, "May you live long, your lordship, winning every battle." And he gave the gift to the king.

The king asked Somadatta, "Somadatta, is this your father?" And Somadatta answered, "Yes, your lordship." Then the father said the verse that he had learned by heart:

"I had two oxen, your lordship, to plough my field.
One died. Take the second one, your lordship."

Hearing this, the king understood that he had made a mistake in reciting one of the words of the stanza, and that instead of saying, "give," he had said, "take." The king laughed loudly, and asked, "Oh Somadatta, are there many oxen at your home like this?"[15] The Enlightenment Being said, "Your lordship, he is guileless. Please give him an ox." And the king, being very pleased that the Enlightenment Being was not trying to gain his ends by using a stratagem, gave the Enlightenment Being's father ten oxen and the village where he lived, and sent them away by a chariot.

As the Enlightenment Being was going with his father on the chariot, he asked his father, "My father, after having spent an entire year learning the verse I taught you while in an isolated and lonely place where there are only fragrant trees, why did you forget what to say?"

The father said, "My son, whether we speak correctly or incorrectly in public, there are always some people who will like whatever we say. Even by saying the wrong thing before the king, I have obtained such wealth."

Saying this, the Buddha ended the story of the Brahmin Somadatta.

15   In South Asia, there is an expression, "to be as foolish as an ox."

"Somadatta's father at that time was this monk Lāḷudāyī. The son Somadatta was I who am today the Buddha."

The moral: "Guileless and simple people get the understanding of those who are compassionate."

$$\boxed{212}$$

The Story of Leftover Food
(*Ucchiṭṭhabhatta-Jātaka*)

When the omnipresent one who was the chief of those having a happy afterlife [*sugata*] was living in Jetavanārāma, he delivered this story with regard to a monk who was confused on account of a woman.

At one time, when King Brahmadatta was ruling the city of Benares, the Enlightenment Being was born in a very poor family of acrobats, and he earned his living by begging alms. At that time, the wife of a certain Brahmin was engaged in adultery.

One day, the Enlightenment Being was going on his alms round, begging alms. In the meantime, the Brahmin husband left his home, going to a nearby village. While he was away, this Brahmin's wife invited her lover in, and the two engaged each other in illicit pleasure. When her lover was ready to leave, she said, "Eat something before you go." She quickly cooked some hot rice and curry. And she gave him the food to eat. While he was eating, she stood at the door and watched to see if her husband was coming. The Enlightenment Being, who was on his alms round, was standing nearby the door, thinking that she might give him some food.[16] At the same time, the Brahmin husband was returning home from having been far away.

When the Brahmin woman saw her householder husband returning home from where he had been, she hurried her lover into the house's storeroom. When her husband entered, she had him sit down at the table, and putting some hot rice and curry on top of the leftover rice and curry, she placed the plate before him. The husband went to eat the rice. But

---

16 Beggars are very observant. They can tell by the actions of the people in a house that they can observe, what is going on in the house.

when he placed his fingers into it, he discovered that the rice on top was hot, but the rice on the bottom was cold. He asked his wife why this was so. She kept silent. The Brahmin asked her this several times. And she, being afraid of telling him the reason, kept silent.

The Enlightenment Being, who was just outside the door, realized that this was her husband and the other man was her lover. He thought, "It would be good to tell the Brahmin what went on inside the house while he was away." And so he called out, "Oh Brahmin, your wife has a lover whom she was feeding. And when you came, she hid him in the storeroom. She has given you food on the same plate, over the food that he was eating. It is my duty, even though I was born in a family of acrobats, to tell you the truth, whether it be good or bad. Demand of your wife not to do wrong things in the future." And he went away.

The Brahmin took both his wife and her lover, beat them, and warned them not to do such things again.

Saying this, the Buddha ended this story about leftover food. At the end of the story the confused monk attained fruit of the stream entrance state of mind that is endowed with a thousand ways to obtain enlightenment.

"This monk at that time was the Brahmin husband. The wife was this woman. And the beggar from the poor acrobat family was I who have become the Buddha."

The moral: "Being righteous is beneficial for everyone."

$$\boxed{213}$$

The Story of King Bharu
(*Bharu-Jātaka*)

When the omnipresent one who is our master and who has a great treasure of kindness towards us was living in Jetavanārāma, he delivered this story with regard to the king of Kosala. The circumstances of this are:

While the omnipresent one was living in Jetavanārāma, he prospered. All his needs and his community's needs were taken care of. His good reputation was known by everyone.

At that time, adherents of other sects [*titthiya*-s], finding that their alms were diminishing, thought, "The revered Gotama and his community of disciples prosper, receiving much alms. And we are getting nothing. They must be prospering and receiving much alms because of the favorable location in which they are dwelling." They thought, "It would be good for us to also build a dwelling near that favorable land. But if we set about building a temple there without telling the king first, the Buddha's disciples will not let us do it. It would be advisable, therefore, to tell the king first, give him a handsome bribe, and get his permission. Thinking so, they offered the king 100,000 gold coins, saying, "Your lordship, we are planning to build a temple for ourselves nearby Jetavanārāma. If the Buddha's disciples come and complain to you about this, please do not stop us." And they made the king promise.

They summoned many carpenters and other workmen, and these began their work, making a lot of noise right next to Jetavanārāma. Hearing all this noise, the Buddha summoned the Venerable Ānanda and found out from him the reason for the noise. He said to the Venerable Ānanda, "Ānanda, summon the community of monks, go to the king, and complain to him about this disturbance." Ānanda and the monks agreed to this. They went together to the palace, and let the king know of their visit.

The king knew why they had come. As he had no favorable answer to give them, he sent a messenger to tell them that he was not at home. The Buddha's disciples then returned to Jetavanārāma and related this to the Buddha. The Buddha understood that the king had been bribed, and he told this to his disciples. The next day, he sent the two chief disciples, Sāriputta and Moggallāna, to complain about what was going on to the king.

The two chief disciples had the king informed of their visit. The king sent the same message as before, that he was not at home.

The next day, the omnipresent one summoned 500 saintly disciples [*arahant*-s], and together they went to the palace. The king came down from his chambers on the upper floor of the palace, knelt down so as to pay respect to the Buddha, took the Buddha's begging bowl, and followed the Buddha into his palace. He fed the Buddha and the 500 Arahants. When they were finished eating, he sat down to the side of the Buddha. Then, the omnipresent one said, "Oh king, in the past, on account of taking bribes, some kings have fallen into disaster." The king then requested that the Buddha disclose the story of old. And the Buddha did so. This is how it was:

At one time in olden days, when King Bharu was reigning in the country of Bharu,[17] the Enlightenment Being was an ascetic living in the Himalayan Mountains together with 500 ascetic followers. During the period of the spring retreat, they wandered here and there.[18] And in due course, they came to the city of Bharu. They collected alms throughout

---

17 So, the Pāli text. The late 13th c. – early 14th c. C.E. translation of the Pāli Jātaka stories into Sinhala by Vīrasimha Pratirāja narrates this story of King Brahmadatta, reigning in the city of Benares, as are other Jātaka stories – probably due to convention.
18 The spring retreat takes place from the full moon of July through the full moon of October, the three months of the rainy season in most of South Asia.

the city, and then left the city through its northern gate. And they took shelter there under a large banyan tree.

After the spring retreat, they went back to the Himalayan forest.

The following year during the spring retreat, they returned again to that place. When they returned, a few of the ascetics who had taken shelter before under a banyan tree at the city's southern gate, which tree had now fallen down on account of all the rain, were now taking shelter under the banyan tree near the city's northern gate. They said, "We were under this banyan tree during the last spring retreat. This is our proper place. Why are you here? We do not want you staying here." And there was a quarrel. The others said, "We came here before you during this spring retreat. We will not leave." So arguing, they went to the king with their quarrel.

The king heard both sides of the story and said, "The place belongs to those ascetics who were there last year." Hearing this decision, the small group of the other ascetics, by their psychic power [*iddhi*], found the golden body of a chariot that belonged formerly to a universal monarch [*cakkavattin*]. They gave it to the king as a bribe, and asked of him to please give them that place. The king then agreed. [Then, the first group of ascetics by their psychic power, found the jeweled wheels of that chariot, and gave that to the king as a bribe. And the king then gave the place to them again.][19] And the two groups of ascetics quarreled.

While they were quarreling, they simultaneously realized that as they had given up the five sensual desires with its cravings when giving up lay life, by giving bribes and quarreling over such a place in this way, they were acting badly and against their own beliefs. Realizing this, both groups of ascetics became very upset and quickly went back to the Himalayan forest.

The divine beings saw this incident, and they became very upset. They thought, "By this king's doing wrongly, and by his conflicting decisions, he created a violation of these ascetics' worldly renunciation.

---

19   The Sinhala translation of the Pāli Jātaka stories by Virasiṁha Pratirāja does not mention this point. The Pāli text does, though.

We ought to punish him and destroy his city." Stirring up the ocean, they sent a big tidal flood [tsunami] and destroyed the kingdom for an area of 300 Yojanas.

Relating this, the Buddha said to King Pasenadi of Kosala, "Oh king, because of one king's wrong deed, many human beings were killed. It is not good to be partial and thereby make bad decisions." In this way, the Buddha warned the king about unjust deeds and ended this story of Bharu.

The king of Kosala, hearing this Dhamma sermon, ordered that the building being done near Jetavanārāma by the adherents of the other sects [*titthiya*-s] be destroyed.

The Buddha then said:

"The chief ascetic in olden times was I who am today the Buddha."

The moral: "It is not good to create conflict among others for the sake of worldly riches."

214

The Story of a River at Flood
(Puṇṇanadī-Jātaka)

When the Buddha, who was like a wish-conferring gem, was living at Jetavanārāma, he delivered this Jātaka story about his perfection of wisdom.

One day, the monks who were gathered in the preaching hall said amongst themselves, "Brethren, the omnipresent one has a great wisdom of understanding the grammatical and etymological explanations of words [niruttipaṭibhāna] and the nature of the world [dhammapaṭibhāna].[20] He has a knowledge that covers everything, as wide as space itself. He has the wisdom of a shining, contented, happy person. He has a sharp, quick, and penetrating reasoning power. Also, he has a quick mind and a discriminating wisdom. He is skillful at stratagems. Whatever situations arise in front of him, he can solve them easily." In this way, they were discussing the Buddha's perfection of wisdom [paññā-pāramī].[21] While they were discussing this, the Buddha entered. The Buddha said, "Oh monks, what were you talking about before I came here?" They said that they were talking about the Buddha's perfection of wisdom. Then the Buddha said, "Now I have obtained an omnipresent state of mind. But even before this, when I was engaged in fulfilling the perfections to become a Buddha as an Enlightenment Being, I was supremely wise enough to have a keen understanding of things." The monks requested the Buddha to disclose a story of olden time. The Buddha then related this story:

---

20 An Arahant who has realized the nature of life has fourfold understandings [catupaṭisambhidā]. These are listed in full in note 1 above.

21 According to the Abhidhamma literature, the Buddha gained 73 wisdoms simultaneously with his enlightenment.

At one time, King Brahmadatta was ruling the city of Benares. At that time, the Enlightenment Being was born as the son of his Brahmin advisor. When the Enlightenment Being grew up, he was sent to Takkasilā to study under a well-known teacher. Studying under him, the Enlightenment Being learned all the disciplines of knowledge of that time. Then, he returned home. And when his father died, he became the king's advisor in this father's place.

Others, who were jealous of the Enlightenment Being, misinformed the king about something they alleged he had done, and on this account the king banished him from the city of Benares. The Enlightenment Being took his wife and children, as well as all his belongings, and went to a certain remote village in the outskirts of the country.

As time went on, the king understood the foolishness of his action, and remembered the Enlightenment Being's good qualities. He thought, "I have done a bad deed by heeding the words of these bad people about such a good man." He decided to bring the Enlightenment Being back into his service. He thought, "It would not be good for me to send a messenger to summon him. So, I will send him a riddle. By means of that riddle, I can summon him." And he formed a riddle. The king composed a poem, and sent this stanza to the Enlightenment Being:

"It is easy to drink from the bank of a river at flood.
When barley ripens, seeds hide in their husks.
One who has gone far from home is invited to return again.
I am sending you as a gift the flesh of an auspicious
being. Please eat it, and read my stanza correctly."

Having written this stanza on a palm leaf, he wrapped it around some crow's meat and sealed it with some lac on which he placed his signature.[22]

---

22   In South Asia, even today, a palm leaf letter is wrapped up in a curl and sealed with some lac. In Sri Lanka, horoscopes written at the time of a baby's birth are also so wrapped up in a curl. But as with other sacred documents these are not sealed with lac, but instead the leaf is cut in such a fashion that it can be closed tightly and re-opened easily again and again.

The Enlightenment Being, having received this stanza, thought about its meaning. The meaning of the first line of the stanza is that when a river is at flood, a crow can drink the water from its perch on the river's bank [*kākapeyya*]. The meaning of the second line is that when barley ripens, the seeds dry up and become smaller, and the husk hides them, whereas when barley is not ripe, the seeds are very large. At such a time, when the barley is ripe, before people can reap it with sickles, some seeds fall on the ground. After the reaping these seeds, hidden under straw, are picked up and eaten by crows. The meaning of the third line is that in such cases, when one returns, a crow acts as a soothsayer.[23] The meaning of the fourth line is that such a being's meat has come to you. Eat of it!

In this way, the Enlightenment Being solved the riddle saying, "In the rainy season, when floods come, crows drink water from their perch. Seeds hidden under straw are eaten by crows. Crows also act as soothsayers. Therefore, oh Brahmin, you have been given this gift of crow meat, and I invite you to return to Benares." Satisfied that he had solved the riddle, he became happy. And he also composed a stanza:

"Your lordship, I have understood that you are compassionate toward me.

By sending me crow's meat, I realize that whenever
you get the meat of swans, herons, peacocks, and like birds,
You also will think about me.
Therefore, I would like to return."

Saying this, [he inscribed it on a palm leaf and sent it back to the king with the messenger. And] he took a decked-out chariot and returned to the city of Benares.

The king, seeing the Enlightenment Being, was happy. He gave the Enlightenment Being his former place as advisor to the king. And the Enlightenment Being lived there happily.

23　In South Asia, a crow is believed to caw when a guest will be arriving from far away.

In this way, the Buddha ended this Jātaka story of a river at flood, and he said:

"At that time, the king was the Venerable Ānanda. And the Brahmin advisor was I who have become the fully enlightened one."

The moral: "If one becomes well educated, he will gain good position."

The Story of a Tortoise
(*Kacchapa-Jātaka*)

When the Buddha, whose renown is comparable to the cosmic tree,[24] was living in Jetavanārāma, he delivered this story about the Venerable Kokālika. The circumstances of its delivery are given in the *Takkāriya-Jātaka* [No. 481]. [For the story as told in the *Takkāriya-Jātaka*, see the *Tittira-Jātaka* (No. 117) in Vol. 3, where the story is given in full.] Here again, the Buddha said, "Oh monks, this monk Kokālika fell to ruin by talking not only now, but also in the past." The monks then asked the Buddha to disclose the old story. The Buddha told the story in this way:

At one time, when Brahmadatta was king of Benares, the Enlightenment Being became one of his ministers.

At that time, the king of Benares was very talkative. The Enlightenment Being thought, "This king talks too much. Whenever I have the opportunity, I will try to put a stop to it."

While he was thinking like this, two swans that lived in the Himalayan forest became friendly with a certain tortoise. One day, they said to their friend the tortoise, "Oh tortoise, we live in a golden cave in the Himalayan forest. That place is interesting to see. Would you like to come there with us to see the place?" The tortoise said, "You can fly! But how can I go there?" The swans said, "If you can keep your mouth shut, we both can carry you." Saying this, they took a stick by both its ends and had the tortoise hold onto it in the middle between his teeth. And they started to fly.

---

24 Ancient India was known as Jambudīpa, the land of the rose apple tree, because there was there a certain rose apple tree that existed at the beginning of this aeon and would exist until the aeon's end. This rose apple tree was referred to as the cosmic tree [*kappaduma*].

As they were flying like this, a group of children who were playing saw this tortoise being carried in this way by the two swans. They shouted, "Look! Two swans are carrying a tortoise in the air." The tortoise heard this, and he wanted to call out to them, "What is it to you if I am being carried through the air by my friends?" Thinking that he would say this, he opened his mouth.

At that time, they were over the streets of the city of Benares. And the tortoise fell there to the ground. Breaking in two, he died. The people in the city noisily clamored, "A tortoise has fallen from the sky and died."

The king heard this news and went to that spot to see for himself what had happened. His ministers also came with him. The king asked the Enlightenment Being, "Why did this tortoise die like this, falling from the sky while he was being carried by two swans?"

The Enlightenment Being thought, "While the two swans were carrying him, the tortoise heard somebody's comments and tried to talk back. This is a good chance to admonish the king not to talk too much. Now I have a way to do that."

He then said, "Your lordship, this tortoise died not knowing how to keep his mouth shut. On account of that, he fell down to this place and died. In the same way, your lordship who is supreme to all your subjects, if someone speaks unnecessarily to others, he will come to the same fate."

Hearing these words, the king said, "Are you referring to me?" Then the minister said, "Yes, your lordship, it apples to everyone." From that time on, the king ceased talking frivolously.

Saying this, the Buddha ended this story of a tortoise.

"At that time, the two swans were the two Venerable chief disciples of the Buddha [Sāriputta and Moggallāna]. The tortoise was the monk Kokālika. The king was the Venerable monk Ānanda. And the minister was I who am today the fully enlightened one who has become the teacher to the three worlds."

The moral: "It is good to control one's words."

(216)

The Story of a Fish
(*Maccha-Jātaka*)

When the omnipresent one who was very compassionate was living in Jetavanārāma, a certain householder became ordained a monk, and he left his wife. Later, he became lovesick for her. This Jātaka story was delivered about him.

The Buddha at one time saw that this monk was confused with regard to his monkhood. He said, "Oh monk, are you confused about your monkhood?" The monk answered, "Yes, your reverence." The Buddha said, "Oh monk, on account of this woman in a previous birth as well, you fell into trouble." The other monks present asked, "How was that, your reverence?" And the enlightened one disclosed the story of the past.

This is how it was:

At one time, Benares was ruled by a king called Brahmadatta. The Enlightenment Being was a Brahmin advisor to that king.

At that time, some fishermen were catching fish using nets. They caught a big fish, and tossing him on the hot sand, they said, "This fish will be good to roast."[25] Saying this, they made a fire and fashioned a wooden spit. In the meantime, the fish's mate was thinking, "It would be no suffering to me if my husband were drying up on the hot sand and was to be impaled on a spit." The fish, on the other hand, was thinking, "If my mate thinks in my absence that I have gone with another female fish, she will suffer." Both thought, "If my mate has gone with another fish, it

---

25 The circumstances leading up to this fish being caught in the net are missing in all versions of this story. It is implied by what follows that he was chasing after his mate, so he did not pay attention to the net, and she did not see what had happened to him.

is that which would make me suffer." And he thought, "If someone could save my life, that would be a good thing." Thinking thoughts like this, they both wept loudly.

At this moment, the Enlightenment Being was there, near the river, thinking he would have a bath. He heard the weeping of the fish. Hearing the painful sound, he begged the fishermen to give him the fish. He then put the fish back in the river, saving his life.

Saying this, the enlightened one ended this Jātaka story of a fish.

"At that time, the female fish was this monk's wife, the male fish was this monk, and the Brahmin who saved the fish's life was I who have now become the fully enlightened one."

The moral: "Love is blind."

The Story of Seggu
(Seggu-Jātaka)

Furthermore, while my lord the omnipresent one was living in Jetavanārāma, he disclosed this Jātaka story with regard to a certain meritorious householder called Paṇṇika.

The circumstances of this story were given in the eleventh decade of stories in the *Paṇṇika-Jātaka* [No. 102]. Here, the householder Paṇṇika went to see the Buddha after having failed to do so for a few days. The Buddha asked him, "Why have you not been here for a few days?" Paṇṇika said, "Oh Venerable sir, I wanted to examine my daughter's virtue and purity, and to arrange her marriage. Because of this, I had to postpone my coming."

The Buddha said, "Not only today, but also in the past, you have examined your faultless daughter in this way." And Paṇṇika invited the Buddha to disclose how it was.

This is how it was:

At one time, when King Brahmadatta was ruling Benares, the Enlightenment Being was born as a tree-spirit in the forest.

A certain householder had a beautiful daughter named Seggu who was pleasant to everyone and who fluttered her eyes in everyone's presence. Because of this, he had doubt about her virginity. And so he wanted to examine her purity before giving her away in marriage.[26] So thinking, he took her with him to the forest. To examine her, he took hold of her hand as if he had lustful thoughts for her. When he did so, his

---

26 Aryan parents protected their children from premarital sex in the belief that were they to have this, the marriage of such people would go wrong and not be successful. The belief was that such people would have no fear of straying from their marital vows.

daughter became afraid of him, and she started to cry. The father then thought, "She is crying now with a cunning mind so as to deceive me." He said, "Why are you crying? The five sensual desires are common to everyone. If you are not a virgin, who do you cry like that?"

Hearing these words, she said, "My respected father, I have never experienced the five sensual desires in such a way. I have never had such an experience of sensual enjoyment. I cried thinking that it is my parents who are my refuge in case of calamity. Should such a calamity come from my parents, to whom am I to complain?" Saying this, she cried even more. And her father then understood that his daughter was blameless and pure. Knowing this, he afterward gave her to an appropriate husband with a lavish celebration.

Saying this, the enlightened one ended the Jātaka story of Seggu.

"The daughter Seggu at that time was this daughter today. The householder was the householder called today Paṇṇika. The tree-spirit [who witnessed this] was I who am today the Buddha."

The moral: "Purity is valued by everyone."

The Story of a Cunning Merchant
(Kūṭavāṇija-Jātaka)

When the Buddha who was the teacher of the whole world was living in Jetavanārāma, this story was disclosed with regard to a certain scheming merchant. These are the circumstances of its telling:

There were two merchants who lived in Sāvatthi. One was very cunning, and the other was very honest and well educated. These two merchants used to carry their wares in bullock carts, one traveling to the east of Sāvatthi and the other traveling to the area to its west. When they would return to the city of Sāvatthi, they would meet together and trade off with one another the remaining wares, depending on what was selling in what region. And they would share their profits with one another. [This went on for a number of years.]

At one point, the cunning merchant thought, "This man, for the entire duration of the last trip, ate only very coarse food and slept in very uncomfortable surroundings. At night, on account of his uncomfortable bed, he has not been able to sleep well and has had to get up a lot. But tonight, after gorging himself on a delicious meal and sleeping the night through in a comfortable bed, he may not be able to properly digest his food and perhaps he will die. When he dies, I can get all his commodities and all his share of the profits." Thinking this, he kept delaying the next trip. And day after day passed.

The honest merchant understood this trick. And next when they divided their goods before preparing to go, he put his mark on all the goods that were his that he was transferring to the cunning merchant. Again, day after day went on.

One evening, the wise merchant took some flowers, incense, and lamps, and he went to see the Buddha. The Buddha saw him and asked, "Why, friend, have I not seen you for a long time? When did you return from your last trip?" Then the merchant said, "Your reverence, I returned two weeks ago." The Buddha asked, "Then why did you not come to see the Buddha?" The merchant explained the reason for his not coming.[27] Hearing the explanation, the Buddha said to him, "Not only now, but even in the past, this man was a cunning rogue." Hearing this, the merchant requested that the Buddha disclose the past story.

This is how it was:

At one time in the past, King Brahmadatta was ruling the kingdom of Benares. At that time, the Enlightenment Being had been born as his Minister of Justice.

Once, a merchant who was living in a remote village came to the city of Benares with iron ploughshares and deposited them with a certain local merchant who was very cunning. He requested that he look after them, keeping them in a safe place. The cunning merchant, rather than keeping them in that safe place, sold them and spent the money as he wanted. And he spread some mouse droppings in the place where the ploughshares had been.

Later, when the village merchant came back to the city of Benares, he went to the cunning merchant and said, "Now, my friend, I need the ploughshares that I gave you to look after." The cunning merchant then said, "Oh, my dear friend, the ploughshares were eaten by mice! See the evidence of it." And he showed him the mouse droppings.

On hearing these words, the village merchant thought, "Ah, is that so? Can mice eat iron ploughshares?" But without saying this, he spoke with the cunning merchant in a friendly fashion. And he requested that the cunning merchant's son come with him to take a bath in a nearby stream. After bathing, he brought the son to another friend's home, left him there, and went back to the cunning merchant's residence.

---

27   The merchant was in the habit of visiting the Buddha before each trip.

The cunning Benares merchant then asked the village merchant, "Where is my son who went to bathe with you?" The village merchant said, "I am sorry! I left your son on the bank of the river and I went to bathe. In the meantime, a hawk snatched him up and flew away. I tried my best to get the hawk to release him, clapping my hands loudly to scare him. But I could not get him to release your son. And he flew off with him."

The Benares merchant said, "Can hawks pick up little children and fly away?" The village merchant said, "What I said, is so. What could I do?" Then the Benares merchant said, "I have no doubt that you have hidden my son somewhere, and are just saying that a hawk took him away. You are lying! I will complain to the Minister of Justice." And he took him to the Minister of Justice and said, "Your lordship, this merchant took my son away with him to bathe, and there is no doubt that he is hiding him somewhere. But he says that a hawk has picked up my son and flown away with him. Please, your lordship, judge my case without being partial."

The Enlightenment Being, who was the judge, asked the village merchant, "Is what he is saying so?" The village merchant said, "Your lordship, what he says is true. But I also have a complaint. Please listen to it."

The village merchant said, "I placed 500 iron ploughshares with him for safekeeping. He said that these ploughshares were eaten by mice. If that is so, and 500 iron ploughshares can be eaten by mice, then his son can be carried off by a hawk. Ask him whether what he said is true. If what he said is so, then there should be no surprise with what I have said."

Hearing this, the Enlightenment Being said, "If this is so, then in response to the deception he told you, you have retaliated with a counter-deception. That is a good retaliation! If iron ploughshares can be eaten by mice, then a child can be carried off by a hawk." And the Enlightenment Being said to the Benares merchant, "If you give him back the iron ploughshares that were eaten by the mice, then he will give you back your son that was carried off by a hawk. If you can agree to your part, he will do his part."

Then the Benares merchant said, "Yes, your lordship, I will give him his 500 ploughshares.[28] Let him give me my son back."

Having concluded this agreement, everything was settled. The village merchant gave the Benares merchant back his son. And the Benares merchant gave the village merchant the 500 iron ploughshares.

Saying this, the Buddha ended this story of a cunning merchant.

"The cunning merchant at that time was the same as today. And the wise merchant was the same as today. The Minister of Justice was I who have today become the fully enlightened one."

The moral: "No matter what the deception, the truth cannot be hidden."

---

28   That is, he will purchase 500 iron ploughshares to replace the ones he had sold, and he will give these to the village merchant.

The Story of Something Ridiculed
(*Garahita-Jātaka*)

When the omnipresent one who became like a mother to the whole world was living in Jetavanārāma, this Jātaka story was disclosed about a monk who was too attached to the sensual desires. These are the circumstances of its disclosure:

At that time, there was a monk who was greedy and was attached to sensual gratification. The other monks knew this, and they brought him to the Buddha and related it. Addressing this monk, the Buddha asked, "Is it true that you have become confused about the practices of a monk in the Buddha's order?" The monk answered, "Yes, your reverence." The Buddha then asked, "What is the reason for this? Why is this so?" The monk responded, "Your reverence, I am drawn to the gratification of the sensual desires." The Buddha said, "Oh monk, even some animals ridicule the five sensual desires." The other monks asked the Buddha to relate how it was. And the Buddha disclosed this story of the past.

This is how it was:

At one time, Benares was ruled by King Brahmadatta. At that time, the Enlightenment Being was born as a monkey. A hunter captured him when he was still young. He took him to the city and gave the young monkey to the king of Benares. The king was very happy and he trained the monkey to do tricks. And the Enlightenment Being, who was the monkey, learned the virtues and the good and bad habits of human beings. And he led a righteous life controlling his senses. The king saw the monkey's virtue, and took compassion on him. He summoned the same hunter who had given the monkey to him and said, "Take this monkey back to the same place where you captured him. Let him go free in the same forest so he can rejoin his family." And the hunter did as the king ordered.

Hearing that the Enlightenment Being had returned, many monkeys gathered to find out from him where he had been. They assembled on a flat rock in the forest and chattering, they asked him, "Where did you go? What have you been doing for such a long time?"

The Enlightenment Being said, "I was captured by a hunter. He took me to the city of Benares and gave me to the king. The king saw my good behavior, became very pleased with me, and requested that same hunter to release me here, back in the forest." The monkeys, hearing this, asked, "What is human behavior like?"

Then the Enlightenment Being said, "What can I say about them! I have nothing to say." He repeated this a couple of times. But the monkeys asked him again and again. Finally, the Enlightenment Being said, "Human beings do not know the impermanence of things, the truth of suffering, and selflessness. They spend their time grasping, saying, 'This is my gold! This is my jewelry! This is my wife! These are my children!' Crying out like this, they pass their time without knowing these three natures of things. Both women and men separate themselves into two groups. Those who have a beard and a moustache are the men. Those who have long breasts, pierced ears, long braids of hair, and who wear jewelry are the women. They divide their society on this basis, and the men marry women with festivity. They then live together in the same home under one roof, but with the women ruling the roost." In this way, the Enlightenment Being explained things as they really were.

The monkeys, hearing these words, held their hands over their ears and said, "Please stop! Please stop! What we have heard is not good to hear." And they named the flat rock on which they had assembled 'Garahitapiṭṭhipāsāṇa,' 'The Flat Rock of Jeering.' And leaving that forest, they went to live in another forest.

Saying this, the omnipresent one ended the *Garahita-Jātaka*, the story of something ridiculed.

"I who am the Buddha at the present time was the chief of those monkeys."

The moral: "Controlling passions is universally respected."

The Story of Dhammaddhaja
[One Who Has Righteousness as His Banner]
(Dhammaddhaja-Jātaka)

One evening, when the omnipresent one who is loved by everyone in the world was living in Jetavanārāma, the monks were talking about Devadatta's attempt to kill the Buddha. At that time, the Buddha came there and said, "Oh monks, what were you talking about before I came here?" The monks told him what they were discussing. Hearing that, the Buddha said, "Oh monks, not only now has Devadatta attempted to kill me, but also in the past he did so. But he could not even daunt my mind." The monks then requested the Buddha to disclose the story. The Buddha then related the story of the past. It was like this:

At one time, King Yasapāni [One Having a Glorious Hand] was ruling Benares.[29] At that time, he had a chief minister named Kāḷaka [The Black One]. He had an attendant named Chattapāṇi [One Who Carries an Umbrella, or Parasol, in His Hand]. And his advisor was the Enlightenment Being who was fulfilling his perfections. His name was Dhammaddhaja.

When his chief minister Kāḷaka was judging cases in court, he used to take bribes. Being partial to the bribe-givers, he would judge cases wrongly.

Once, someone whose case was wrongly judged by him, holding head in hands and crying out loudly against him while on the road, was

---

29 So, the generally adopted Pāli text based here on Burmese manuscripts. Thai manuscripts of the commentary attributed to Buddhaghosa also read Yasapāni. The Sinhala script manuscripts of the commentary read Pāyāsapāṇi [One Who Holds Milkrice (as an Offering) in His Hollowed Hand]. The late 13th – early 14th c. C.E. Sinhala translation of the Pāli Jātaka stories by Virasimha Pratirāja simply gives Brahmadatta as the name of the king here, as elsewhere.

met by the Enlightenment Being who was on the way to the palace. This man fell down in front of the Enlightenment Being and told what the minister Kālaka had done to him, saying, "Kālaka is accepting bribes. And on this account, he wrongly judged my case. Even though the king has such righteous advisors as you, his chief minister is wrongly judging cases. So I have been defrauded, and lost wealth. This is not good!"

The Enlightenment Being heard this and out of his compassion, he asked the man to return to the court with him. There, he reheard the case. Being impartial, he gave a correct judgment. He gave the wealth to the correct owner. The people who had gathered at the court and witnessed this righteous judgment expressed their appreciation of it by calling out loudly, "*Sādhu, sādhu, sādhu.* [Well done! Well done! Well done!]"

The king heard this clamor and wanted to know what it was about. One of his ministers said, "The chief minister, Kālaka, had misjudged a case. But your advisor, Dhammaddhaja, has correctly judged it with impartiality. Many people heard his decision. What you heard was their expressing their appreciation."

The king heard this and summoned the Enlightenment Being into his presence. He said, "Oh advisor, I have heard that you have done a very good deed. Is this so?" The Enlightenment Being answered, "Yes, your lordship." Then the king said, "From today on, you be the judge instead of Kālaka, and solve people's cases." But the Enlightenment Being did not accept his appointment. Again and again, the king requested that he do so. Finally, the Enlightenment Being accepted the appointment to judge people's complaints. From that day on, the Enlightenment Being impartially judged all cases, decreeing owners to be owners and those who were not the owners to be those who were not the owners.

When the Enlightenment Being began to judge the cases in this way, impartially and righteously, the chief minister Kālaka lost his income from bribery. Grieving about his loss, he thought, "If I can cause the king to lose his high opinion of Dhammaddhaja, I can get the king to kill him." Thinking this, he went to see the king. He said, "Your lordship, the erudite advisor Dhammaddhaja is plotting to take your kingdom." The king said, "Advisor, I do not believe that." Then Kāḷaka said, "Your lordship, if you do not believe what I am telling you, tomorrow morning go to the window to look out over the city and observe the splendid way in which he comes surrounded by crowds. Then you will believe me."

The king did as Kāḷaka said. The next morning, he looked out over the city through his window and watched. When the Enlightenment Being was coming, people surrounded him and spoke to him about their cases. The king saw that he was surrounded by many well-disposed people, and he decided that the minister Kāḷaka was correct. Believing this, he asked Kāḷaka, "What should we do now?" The minister Kāḷaka said, "Put him to death, your lordship."

The king said, "How can we put him to death without having found him guilty of some fault?" Hearing the king, the minister said, "There is a stratagem that we can use to do so. Ask him to do a service that he will not be able to do. When he is unable to do it, then we can put him to death." Then the king asked, "What sort of service can we ask him to do?" Kāḷaka said, "Your lordship, it takes three or four years for someone to make a pleasure garden. It cannot be created immediately. So we will ask him to make a pleasure garden within one day. When he fails to do it, we can have him put to death at that time."

After hearing these words, the king summoned the Enlightenment Being and said, "Erudite Dhammaddhaja, I want to sport in a pleasure garden tomorrow. But the present one is old. I want a new garden for tomorrow. When I come here, you must have made a new pleasure garden, or else I will put you to death."

The Enlightenment Being understood that without doubt, this was the work of the minister Kāḷaka. Thinking this, he said, "Yes, your lordship, if it is possible, I will do it." And he went home. He took a bath, washing his head, ate his meal, and sat down on his bed, full of anguish. Then the seat of the king of the gods, Sakka, became hot on account of the power of the Enlightenment Being's virtuousness. Sakka, the king of the gods, looked at the human world with his thousand eyes of wisdom to see who was trying to take by force his splendor. What he saw was that the Enlightenment Being was in difficulty, and was anguished. Seeing him, he thought, "I will have to go there and get him out of his difficulty." Thinking this, he went to the Enlightenment Being's chamber and appeared there mid-air.

The Enlightenment Being asked, "Who are you?" Then Sakka said, "I am the chief of the two divine worlds, the god Sakka. I came here by the power of your virtuousness. I want to know why you are full of anguish." The Enlightenment Being said, "I was asked by my lordship to make a new pleasure garden for him by tomorrow, when he wants to come to sport in it. But it takes at least two or three years to make a pleasure garden. Since this is the case, how can I make one in one day? Thinking about this, I became full of anguish." Then the god Sakka said, "Great being, do not be anguished. Before the morning, I will make a pleasure garden for you that is as beautiful as my pleasure gardens Nandā and Cittalatā. Tell me where you want me to make it." The Enlightenment Being said, "I would like you to make it for me in such-and-such a place." And he gave Sakka the directions to the place, saying, "Our king would like it in that location."

The god Sakka made an 18 *hattha* [forearm lengths] high wall, and inside it, he created mango, rose apple, and the like trees with flowers and fruits. And he returned to his city.

In the morning, the Enlightenment Being had his breakfast, and then he went to see the newly created pleasure garden. Satisfied, he went to see the king and said, "Your lordship, the pleasure garden is ready. You can go there now and enjoy it." Then the king went to see the pleasure garden, looked all about, and satisfied, he said to the minister Kālaka, "He has fashioned a beautiful pleasure garden! Now what are we to do?"

Then Kālaka said, "If the erudite Dhammaddhaja can create a pleasure garden so quickly, let us have him also create in it a well so that we may drink fresh water. And ask him further to create in it a lake adorned by the five types of lotuses and endowed with the seven precious stones by the time your lordship comes to the pleasure garden this evening."

The king agreed, and he summoned the Enlightenment Being. He said, "Erudite, you have fashioned a very beautiful pleasure garden. Now, by this evening, create in it a well so that we may drink fresh water and a lake adorned by the five types of lotuses and endowed with the seven precious stones. If you do not do it by this evening, I will put you to death."

The Enlightenment Being said, "Yes, your lordship, I will do it, if I am able to do so." And, as before, Sakka created in the pleasure garden a large lake endowed with a thousand recesses and with its rippling waters shimmering with the colors of the seven precious stones lining it, embellished by the variegated colors of the five types of lotuses.

The next morning, the Enlightenment Being went to see the pleasure garden, and he saw there the beautiful lake created by Sakka, the king of the gods. He then went to the king and said, "Your lordship, the lake has been completed. You may now go to see it."

The king agreed to this, and went to see the lake. And he was satisfied with what he saw. He said to Kāḷaka, "The lake was created as we requested! Now, what can we do?" The minister Kāḷaka said, "Your lordship, ask him to create a pavilion that is appropriate for such a garden and lake." Then the king summoned the Enlightenment Being and said, "What you have done is very good. Now make an ivory pavilion that is fit for such a garden and lake. If you fail to do it, you will be put to death."

The Enlightenment Being said, "Yes, your lordship, if it is possible, I will do it." Again, Sakka, the king of gods, created it during the night. And the Enlightenment Being viewed it in the morning, then went to see the king, and said, "Your lordship, the pavilion is completed. Please go and see it."

The king went there, and after seeing the pavilion, he said to Kāḷaka, "Oh minister, now what can we do?" Kāḷaka said, "Your lordship, tell him to light the pavilion without lamps, but by the splendor of jewels."

Then the king summoned the Enlightenment Being and said, "Create jewels such that the pavilion can be lit by them, instead of by lamps." That also was so created by the king of gods. The Enlightenment Being saw this as well, and reported it to the king. "Your lordship, the jewels you requested are created." The king went there, saw the pavilion being lit by the splendor of jewels, and said to Kālaka, "What can we do now?"

The minister Kālaka said, "Your lordship, this man does everything that we ask. There is no doubt that he is doing these things by the power of a divine being. So, your lordship, we will have to order him to create as a guard keeper for the pleasure garden a man who has four powers [*caturaṅga-samannāgata-purisa*].[30]

The king heard this, and agreed. He summoned the Enlightenment Being and said, "It is very good that you have created what you have, the pleasure garden, the lake, the pavilion, and the gems. For the protection of them all, now create a guardian keeper endowed with four powers."

The Enlightenment Being said, "Yes, your lordship, if I can do it, I will do it." In this way, he agreed to do it. He then went home, took a bath, and ate a meal. And he started to think, "All the things that have been created so far, have been created by the god Sakka, as he could do them. But there is not among human beings a person with four powers. It is not good to die by the hands of others. It would be better to die as a person who has no refuge. Therefore, I will go into the forest and die there. Dying in the forest as a person who has no refuge would be a good thing." Thinking this, and without informing anyone at his home, he went down from the upper floor of his house and went out the back door, leaving for the forest. There, sitting down under a tree, he thought about the eight vicissitudes of the world. These are gain and loss, fame and disgrace, blame and praise, happiness and unhappiness. While he was so thinking, the god Sakka became aware of what the Enlightenment Being had done. He came to the place where the Enlightenment Being was, disguised as a hunter, and said, "Revered one, from your appearance, you were living happily at home. Why are you now sitting homeless in the forest?" The Enlightenment Being said, "That is true, hunter! I was happy

---

30   According to Buddhaghosa, such a man does not exist in the world, so no one knows what his four powers are.

at home. And now I am alone in the forest." Then Sakka, the hunter, asked, "Why, then, are you now alone in the forest?" The Enlightenment Being disclosed to him everything that had happened in the city with the king. He then said further, "Now the king has asked me to create a human being who is endowed with four powers to protect the pleasure garden. That cannot be done not only by me, but even by a divine being. It is not good to die helplessly at the hands of another in the city. It would be better to die here in the forest."

The king of gods, Sakka, after listening to him, said, "Why, your lordship, do you mistake me as a hunter. I am the king of gods, Sakka, who created for you whatever you needed in the city again and again. While I am helping you in this way, why did you want to come here like this? While such as I exist, doing for you whatever you ask, there is no need for you to be forlorn. It is true that a human being with four powers cannot be created, but I will devise for you a stratagem. Your king's barber, named Chattapāṇi, is endowed with four powers. Take him to the king, and let the king make him the pleasure garden's keeper.

The Enlightenment Being agreed to this, and he returned home. There, he took a good night's sleep. The next morning, while he was coming to see the king in the palace, he met on his way the barber, Chattapāṇi. He asked him, "Hey, Chattapāṇi, are you endowed with four powers?" Chattapāṇi responded, asking him, "Who said to you that I am endowed with four powers?" The Enlightenment Being said, "The god Sakka told me." Chattapāṇi asked, "Where did you see the god Sakka?" Then the Enlightenment Being told him the whole story of the situation that he was in. Then Chattapāṇi said, "Yes, sir, I am indeed endowed with four powers."

The Enlightenment Being took Chattapāṇi by the hand, went with him to the palace, and bringing him into the king's presence, said, "Your lordship, this man is endowed with four powers. Take this man as guardian of the pleasure garden." Then the king asked, "Is it true, Chattapāṇi, that you are endowed with four powers?"

"Yes, your lordship," he answered. "I am endowed with four powers."
The king said, "Tell me, then, what are your four powers." Chattapāṇi said,
"Your lordship, I do not get angry with anyone, I do not drink alcohol, I
have no strong attachments, and I meditate on loving kindness. These are
my four powers."

The king said, "Everyone in the world has anger [*kodha*] at something.
How can you say that you never get angry?" Then the barber Chattapāṇi
said, "I was born as a king in the past. Listening to the word of my queen,
I imprisoned my Brahmin advisor.[31] From that point on, I gave up having
anger in my mind toward anyone."

The king asked, "How did it happen that you gave up your anger?"

Chattapāṇi then said, "At one time, I was King Brahmadatta in this
country. I had to go on a journey away from the palace. I sent messengers
back to the palace 64 times to inquire after the well-being of the queen.
She engaged in adultery with each of these messengers. And after all
this, when my chief Brahmin advisor just touched her hand, she falsely
accused him to his face of trying to sleep with her. Saying to him that
she would never do such a thing, angrily she stormed out of the room.
She later complained to the king that his chief Brahmin advisor had tried
to molest her. When the king had returned to the palace and heard this
from her, he believed her and had his chief Brahmin advisor arrested.
With his hands being bound behind his back, the king had him brought
to him at the royal court. There the king questioned him as to whether
or not this was true. The advisor said, 'Your lordship, I never did such an
unwholesome deed. Such ought never be done. But I believe that such
was done by each of the messengers you sent back to the queen.'

"The king understood what had really happened, and became angry
with the queen. But the Brahmin advisor said further, 'Your lordship, do
not be angry with the queen. Such is the nature of some women. It would

---

31   This story is told in full in the *Bandhanamokkha-Jātaka*, Jātaka No. 120, but
     from the vantage of the Enlightenment Being. It is here told from the
     vantage of the king.

be like getting angry at dirt that comes from the body, such as sweat, urine, and feces, after one eats good food. Such is natural. One cannot get angry at the food. In the same way, it is not good to get angry with women. Such is their nature.'

"From the time I heard this from my chief Brahmin, I decided not to get angry with anyone until I attain final release from the cycle of re-becoming [*nibbāna*]. On account of this decision, I also do not get angry with anyone in this life."

Then King Yasapāṇi said, "That is all very good. But then why do you not drink alcohol?" The barber Chattapāṇi said, "Your lordship, once long ago I was born as another king. I became intoxicated with toddy, killed my own innocent and playful young son who was very much loved by me, and ate his flesh. From that time on, I have given up the habit of drinking alcohol."

"This is how it was:

"At one time, I was born as a king named Chattapāṇi in this very same country. I never ate my rice without meat and fish. One day, the palace chef realized that as the following day was the full moon day, animals and fish would not be killed. Thinking so, he purchased in advance some meat and placed it in a safe place for the king's meal the following day. Somehow, it got eaten by dogs.

"The chef, being afraid of serving the king rice without fish or meat, went to the queen and said, 'Your grace, the king does not like to eat his rice without fish or meat. On this account, I purchased some meat for the king yesterday and put it aside in a safe place. But it got eaten by dogs. I am afraid of serving the king rice without meat. What can I do?'

"The queen said, 'Do not be afraid on that account. I have a stratagem. The king loves my son very much. When it is time to serve the king his meal, I will bring my son finely decked out to the king and place him on his lap. The king then will not notice whether or not there is meat with his rice, because he will have all his attention placed on his son.'

"The royal chef said, 'That is good.'

"When it was time for the king to have his lunch, he drank some toddy and became intoxicated. At that time, the queen brought his son and placed him on the king's lap. While the king was eating, he noticed nevertheless that there was no meat with his rice. He questioned, 'Hey chef, why is there no meat today?' The chef said, 'Your lordship, I am afraid to tell you why! Yesterday, I purchased meat for you and placed it in a safe place. But it was eaten by dogs. As today is the full moon day, there is no meat being sold in the market. So none can be bought.' The king then got upset and said, 'You may not have any meat at hand, but I have meat.' Saying this, he snapped the neck of his young baby son and handed him to the chef, saying, 'Go and cook this meat, and bring it to me.'

"The chef did not argue with him, but just did as he said. He cooked the meat, and served the king. The king then ate his beloved son's flesh. No one dared say anything. The king ate, was satisfied with his meal, washed his hands and rinsed his mouth, and went to sleep. When he woke up and was no longer intoxicated, he requested that his young son be brought to him.

"Then the queen fell at the king's feet crying. The king asked her, 'Why are you crying like this?' The queen said, 'Oh my lord, do you not remember what happened at lunchtime? You ate your son's flesh with your rice.' Hearing this, he became very upset and thought, 'Oh, what have I done because of my fault of drinking toddy!' Having become very upset, he decided, 'From this time on, I will not drink alcohol until I obtain final release from the cycle of re-becoming [*nibbāna*].' On account of that decision, I do not drink alcohol even today."

Then King Yasapāṇi said, "That is all very good. But then why do you not have any strong attachments to anyone?"

The barber Chattapāṇi said, "At one time, I was a king who was the father of a son who committed the crime of breaking the begging bowl of a Pacceka-Buddha.[32] I became sad that I was the father of such a son

---

32   A Pacceka-Buddha, or 'silent Buddha', is a Buddha who has attained supreme and perfect insight but dies without proclaiming the truth to the world.

who had fallen into hell. For that reason, I decided to no longer have attachment to anyone in this world."

The king then asked for the story in detail. This is how it was:

"At one time, I was a king called Kitavāsa in this city. A son was born to me. The soothsayers said at that time when they saw my son, 'Your lordship, this son will die one day without having any water to drink.' Hearing this, the king had made four lakes outside the four gates of the city. Even inside the city, he made large and small wells and ponds everywhere, and he made sure that there was drinking water everywhere. Time passed.

"The young prince grew up and became the secondary king of the country. He was named Duṭṭhakumāra [One Who is a Wicked Young Man]. The king loved him very much. He used to take him along with the rest of the family wherever he went, as if they were his own shadow.

"One day, Duṭṭhakumāra mounted an elephant and taking the fourfold army, without his father he went on a procession around the city. At that time, a Pacceka-Buddha who was very virtuous and who had gained control of his six faculties of sense came onto the street in front of the procession, holding his begging bowl with some rice in it. The multitude that had gathered to watch the procession, seeing him, instead began to pay reverence to him and to appreciate his virtuousness.

"The secondary king thought, 'Seeing such a person as me, why are these people instead of paying me respect, paying respect to this bald-headed monk?' He got angry at him, and dismounting his elephant, he approached the Pacceka-Buddha and asked, 'Have you gotten enough rice to eat in your begging bowl?' The Pacceka-Buddha said, 'Yes, your lordship.' Hearing that, Duṭṭhakumāra said, 'Let me see.' And he took the bowl in his hand, placed it on the ground, and stomped on it, breaking it into pieces.

"Then the Pacceka-Buddha looked at him, thinking, 'For no reason, this prince has unwholesome thoughts toward me.' The prince thought, on looking at the Pacceka-Buddha's face, that he was angry with him.

He said with anger, 'Do you not know that I am the son of King Kitavāsa, known as Duṭṭhakumāra? You can do nothing to me by getting angry.' That day, the Pacceka-Buddha had nothing to eat. He left the city and went to the foot of the Nanda rock to the north [in the Himalayan Mountains].

"At that time, flames rose out of the great hell called Avici and setting on fire the body of the prince, he became very hot and requested water.[33] Meanwhile, all the lakes, ponds, and wells in the city dried up from the heat of Avici's flames. And the ground where the prince was, opened up, and the prince was swallowed up.

"I, myself, King Kitavāsa, became very upset and became consumed with grief. I thought, 'Through attachment to someone, there arises in the mind great suffering and many bad thoughts. On that account, from this time, I will not have attachment to anything or anyone until I attain final release from the cycle of re-becoming [*nibbāna*]."

King Yasapāṇi heard these words and said, "That is all very good. But why do you practice loving kindness toward everyone?"

The barber Chattapāṇi said that he was once born as an ascetic who practiced loving kindness toward everyone. He said, "Long ago, I was born in this city with the name Araka.[34] I practiced meditation on loving kindness, and was afterward born in the Brahma world, where I lived for seven aeons [*kappa*-s, Skt. *kalpa*-s]. During all that time, I practiced loving kindness. As a result of that practice, even now I have the power from loving kindness that I can spread toward all beings."

King Yasapāṇi heard these words and thought, "There is no doubt that there is no reason for me to be upset with the erudite Dhammaddhaja. On account of the minister Kālaka lying to me because he was no longer able to get bribes, I have become unjustly upset with Dhammaddhaja." Thinking this, he glared at Kālaka. All the ministers, on seeing the face of the king, understood that the king was angry with Kālaka. They said, "The

---

33   The flames of Avici do not consume what they burn, but cause one to suffer with the sensation of burning.

34   See the *Araka-Jātaka*, Jātaka No. 169. Araka there, though, was the Enlightenment Being.

bribes that you have taken through the years are finished with now." And they set upon Kāḷaka and knocked him to the ground. They then threw him out of the palace into a refuse heap, where a multitude of citizens hit him with whatever they could pick up.

Saying this, the Buddha ended the story of the erudite Dhammaddhaja.

"The minister Kāḷaka at that time is the monk Devadatta. And the erudite Dhammaddhaja was I who have today become the Buddha."

The moral: "Good practice always brings good results. Bad practice always brings bad results."

The Story of a Yellow Robe
(Kāsāva-Jātaka)

When the Buddha who assists the whole world was living in Jetavanārāma, he delivered this Jātaka story about Devadatta. The origin of this story took place at Veḷuvanārāma, the Bamboo Grove temple.

At one time, when the Venerable Sāriputta was living at Veḷuvanārā-ma, the devotees of that village [Rājagaha] were organizing to give alms [dāna] to the Venerable Sāriputta and Devadatta.

At the time, a wealthy businessman from outside the village contributed for the purpose of the almsgiving a perfumed cloth worth 100,000 gold coins. After all the other alms had been given, this cloth still remained. The organizers of the almsgiving then discussed to whom this cloth should be given, the Venerable Sāriputta or Devadatta. Some of them said, "We will give this to the Venerable Sāriputta." Others said, "Let us give this to the Venerable Devadatta." Some said, "Venerable Sāriputta will remain here for two or three days, and then go. He will not be with us through our happiness and unhappiness. It is not the same with Devadatta. He will stay here like a hidden treasure, and will care about our happiness and unhappiness.[35] Because of this, he deserves to get this cloth." And with a unanimous decision, they gave Devadatta the cloth.

The Venerable Devadatta cut the cloth into pieces, had it sewn together, and had it hemmed.[36] He then had it dyed the bright yellow color of a Kaṇikāra flower. And he always went about proudly wearing this robe as it had been given to him, and not to the Venerable Sāriputta.

---

35   Gayāsīsa, where Devadatta dwelt with 500 monks, was nearby Rājagaha.
36   The fabric for monks' robes is cut into pieces that are then sewn together and hemmed, so that thieves will not steal the fabric for sale.

While time was passing in this way, some 30 monks from Veḷuvanā-rāma went to see the Buddha at Jetavanārāma. The Buddha asked for the latest news. They said, "Venerable sir, the Venerable Devadatta sports a robe that is not suitable to him, but rather to an Arahant." And the Buddha said, "Oh monks, not only now, but even in the past, Devadatta has worn the garb of an Arahant when it was not suitable to him." The monks said, "Venerable sir, we do not know that story. Please tell it." And the Buddha told this story of the past:

At one time, King Brahmadatta was ruling in Benares. At that time, the Enlightenment Being had been born as the chief of 80,000 elephants in the Himalayan forest. With him as the chief of the elephants, they wandered about the forest.

Once, a poor man who lived in Benares went to the street where the ivory carvers lived. While he was talking with them, they told him that if he could bring them ivory, he could earn a lot of money. Considering this, he figured he would be able to get ivory in the forest. He thought, "If I go like this, the elephants will kill me. But if I disguise myself as a Pacceka-Buddha, they will not kill me. And I can get ivory by killing one of them." Thinking so, he disguised himself as a Pacceka-Buddha and went to the forest. He sat beside a path by which the elephants went, hiding a weapon under his robe. The elephants, seeing him and thinking that he was a Pacceka-Buddha, reverently knelt down before him and went on.

The hunter, using his weapon, killed the last elephant in the herd to pass by. He cut off the elephant's tusk, and sold the ivory to the ivory carvers. In this way, he began to earn a good deal of money.

As time passed, the elephants in the herd noticed that their numbers were dwindling. They mentioned it to their chief. Hearing this, the Enlightenment Being thought that there was no doubt that the man who was sitting beside the road dressed as a Pacceka-Buddha was in fact an elephant hunter. Thinking he would ascertain this for sure, one day he went behind the rest of the herd.

On that day, the man who was disguised as a Pacceka-Buddha was sitting in the same way as before, on the side of the road. Seeing the last elephant in the herd pass by, the hunter took out his weapon and struck. Then the elephant immediately caught the man with his trunk, picked him up, and wanted to smash him on the ground. Before doing so, though, he thought, "Whether he is a hunter or not, he is wearing a yellow robe which is worthy of an Arahant. Therefore, out of respect for what he is wearing, it is not good to kill him." He said, "Hey sinful man, it is not proper for people like you to wear such noble garb that is worthy of an Arahant. You, by sitting here in this way, have killed a large number of elephants in my herd. If I see you sitting here any more, remember what I was just now going to do to you." Warning him in this way, he sent him away without killing him.

In this way, the Buddha ended the Jātaka story of a yellow robe.

"The hunter at that time was the monk Devadatta. And the chief of the elephants was I who am today the fully enlightened Buddha."

The moral: "You can't judge a book by its cover."

The Story of Cūlanandiya (or, Cūlanandaka)[37]
(Cūlanandiya-Jātaka, Cūlanandaka-Jātaka)

When the omnipresent one was living in the Bamboo Grove temple [Veḷuvanārāma], this story *was* told about Devadatta.

One day, the elderly monks who were assembled in the preaching hall in the evening said, "The Venerable Devadatta tried to kill the Buddha without any mercy by using archers, and in many other ways. Even though seeing the Buddha's compassion, virtue, and wisdom, he had no compassion toward the Buddha, and could not generate any compassion toward the Buddha. Because of his unwholesome qualities, he is a very callous man." While they were talking in this way, the Buddha entered and asked, "Oh monks, what were you talking about before I came?" The monks told him they were discussing the callous nature of Devadatta. The Buddha said, "Oh monks, not only now, but even before Devadatta was callous like this." The monks then requested the Buddha to relate the story of the past. The Buddha disclosed the past story of Devadatta in this way:

At one time, there was a king called Brahmadatta in Benares. When he was ruling the country, the Enlightenment Being was born in the Himalayan forest as the chief of 80,000 monkeys. He was known as Nandiya. He had a younger brother who was known as Cūlanandiya [Small Nandiya]. These two brothers looked after their blind and elderly mother.

The Enlightenment Being and his brother would go out in search of food together with other monkeys of the troop. When they found ripe fruit and yams, they would eat some themselves, and send some back to their mother with other monkeys. These other monkeys, though, did not

---

37   This Jātaka story is referred to in 'The Questions of King Milinda' (*Milinda-pañha*) 4.4.24.

deliver the fruit and yams to the mother, but ate them themselves. In the course of time, the mother became very weak and lean because she did not have enough food to eat.

One day, the Enlightenment Being asked his mother, "Why are you so weak and lean? I have been sending back to you much food to eat." The mother said, "Oh my son, no one has given me any of the food that you are sending."

Hearing this unfortunate news, the Enlightenment Being said to his younger brother, Cūlanandiya, "I am not able to properly look after our blind and elderly mother while leading this troop of monkeys. Therefore, let me leave the troop, and you become their chief." The brother said, "No! I have no desire to be the chief of the troop. I, too, will look after our mother." So, the Enlightenment Being and his brother both decided to leave the troop of monkeys.

Taking their mother, they went toward the city of Benares. And, on the boundary of the city, they made a home in a very big banyan tree. They lived there, taking care of their mother.

In the meantime, a young man went to Takkasilā to receive his education from the most famous teacher in the city at that time. The teacher understood the young man's poor temperament and thought, "What is the advantage of teaching this man? He is a bad person." Then again, he thought, "This man exerts a great deal of effort in whatever he undertakes. Let me educate him." Thinking so, he taught him many subjects. And after he had finished, he advised him not to do anything rash, not to hurt anybody, not to do any bad deeds, and gave him many other admonitions. And he sent him home.

The man listened to his teacher's advice, and went back to Benares. Once there, he took a bow and arrows, and started to hunt for living animals. Selling their meat, he earned a living. One day, he was unable to find any living animals and was returning home in the evening empty handed. On the boundary of the city, he saw a huge banyan tree. When he came under the tree, he looked up and saw the Enlightenment Being, along with his brother, helping their mother. He decided to try to kill them with his bow and arrows. The Enlightenment Being, seeing this, thought, "As my mother is so old, and so very weak and thin, this man will not kill her." The hunter thought, seeing the old she-monkey, "I will kill her, and let my children eat her." He raised his bow and arrow toward her.

The Enlightenment Being thought, "This hunter is trying to kill my mother." Thinking this, he resolved to give his life in his mother's stead. He said to the hunter, "Please let my mother live! In her stead, I will give you my life. Letting her live, kill me and eat my flesh." The hunter said, "I will give your mother the gift of life [*jīvita-dāna*]." Saying this, he shot his arrow at the Enlightenment Being and killed him.

After killing him, he again raised his bow to kill the mother. Then the Enlightenment Being's younger brother thought, "This hunter is trying to kill my mother. Rather than let her die, I will give my life in her stead. Even if she lives only one day more, that would be better than letting her die today." Thinking so, he came up to the hunter and said, "You killed my brother. Kill me also. The flesh of the two of us will be enough for today. Let our mother live." The hunter agreed to this, and killed the Enlightenment Being's younger brother. Then he decided again to kill the mother, thinking again, "Her flesh will be good for my children to eat." And he shot his arrow at the blind she-monkey.

Taking the carcasses of the three monkeys on a carrying pole, he set out for home. At that moment, a thunderbolt hit his home, setting it on fire, and his wife and two children died in the blaze. When he heard this news, he dropped his bow and arrows on the ground and dropped the pole with the monkey carcasses on the ground. Becoming as a mad person, he tore his clothing off and placed it over his shoulder. And he ran to his home. When he entered what remained of his home, a burnt timber fell on him. At that moment, the earth opened, creating a chasm out of which there came flames that engulfed his body, and he fell into hell.

While he was falling into hell, he recalled what his teacher said to him, "Do not do anything that causes misfortune." He said to himself, "I have seen the result of violating that admonition today. If someone does a bad deed, the same thing happens to himself. If someone does a good deed, he receives the results of that good deed in kind. Whatever seeds someone sows, he reaps fruit of the same kind." Saying this to himself, he fell into the fire-burning hell.

In this way, the Buddha finished disclosing the Jātaka story of Cūlanandiya.

"The hunter at that time was Devadatta. The teacher was the Venerable Sāriputta. The Enlightenment Being's mother was the Venerable nun Pajāpatī Gotamī. The younger brother Cūlanandiya was the Venerable Ānanda. And the chief of the monkeys was I who have become the enlightened Buddha."

The moral: "Bad deeds have bad results and good deeds have good results."

223

The Story of a Packet of Food
(Puṭabhatta-Jātaka)

While the Buddha who became a virtuous friend to the whole world was living in Jetavanārāma, this Jātaka story was delivered on account of a householder. This is how it happened:

One householder who was living in a remote village borrowed money from another householder who lived in Sāvatthi. When the householder who lived in Sāvatthi went to the remote village to collect the debt, the two argued, the householder from the remote village saying he could not pay it at that time. There was a big quarrel. Then, when the householder from the remote village asked the Sāvatthi householder to eat something, the latter, being angry, left with his wife without eating.

On their way back to Sāvatthi, a certain man who was also traveling on the road saw the couple and noticed how lean with hunger their faces were. He gave his packet of food into the householder's hand.[38] The householder thought that he would eat the food all by himself, without giving any to his wife. Thinking this, he said to his wife, "There are robbers in this forest. So, you go first, and I will follow behind."[39] The wife believed what he said, and she went ahead.

Meanwhile, the householder opened the packet of food and ate all the rice. When he caught up with his wife, he said, "Look at the food packet that was given us. The man gave it to us empty, after he had eaten

---

38 When people would go on a journey, it was the custom to take a packet of rice wrapped in an areca nut leaf for nourishment during their travels.

39 When people went by walking in ancient times, it was the practice of thieves and robbers to attack the last person in a group. See, for instance, the stories in the *Biḷāra-Jātaka* [No. 128], the *Aggika-Jātaka* [No. 129], and the *Kāsāva-Jātaka* [No. 221] for comparable situations.

all the food." Hearing this, the wife said, "I saw the food packet that was given to you. You ate all the rice by yourself. After eating it all alone, you are showing me the empty packet." Saying this, she got angry. But out of fear, she remained with him and they arrived together at the city of Sāvatthi. When they came near Jetavanārāma, they saw the pond near the temple. Thinking they would drink the water and wash their feet, they decided to go to see the Buddha.

When the Buddha saw them, he said to the wife, "Lay sister, it appears that you have no affection for your husband." The woman said, "Your reverence, I have love for him, but he has not even a little love for me. For instance, today, on our way here, someone gave us a packet of food. Even though I was hungry, he ate it alone, gave me nothing, and made up a story about it. This is the love he has for me." The Buddha said, "Lay sister, not only today, but even in the past, you have had affection for him, but he showed not even a little affection for you." Saying this, the Buddha said further, "But when a wise person made him realize your worth, then he paid you proper respect." The people who were present at that time then requested the Buddha to tell the story of the past, and he disclosed the story.

At one time, King Brahmadatta was ruling in the city of Benares. The Enlightenment Being at that time was one of the king's advisors. On account of conflict between the king's eldest son and the Enlightenment Being, the king sent his son away from the city. The son took his wife and left the city, going to a remote village in the state of Kāsi. They lived there anonymously as villagers.

After a long time, the king died. When his son heard this news, he decided to return to Benares to take over the kingdom. When he and his wife were about to leave, some villagers gave them a packet of food, saying, "The two of you can eat this on the way." But on their way, the son ate the entire packet of rice alone, and did not give any to his wife. The wife did not say anything, but just thought that he was a very cruel man. And she became very upset with her plight.

When they came to the city of Benares, the son received the kingdom, and he kept her as his chief queen. Thinking that this was enough honor for her, he showed her no other consideration, and he never asked her about her wishes.

The Enlightenment Being, seeing this, one day thought, "This queen has been very helpful to our king. But the king never thinks about her needs. Therefore, it would be meritorious for me to do something on her behalf." Thinking this, one day the Enlightenment Being went to see the queen. He addressed her respectfully, and she asked, "Why, sir, did you come?" He said, "Madam, it is our duty to help those superior to us, such as parents and grandparents. But just as we must help you, you must give to us. [Right now, neither of us is helping one another.]" Then the queen said, "What can I give to you, my son? The king gives me nothing. Even when we were coming for him to take the kingship, people gave us a packet of food to eat on the way. The king ate it all by himself, and did not give me even a bit." Then the Enlightenment Being who was the minister asked, "Madam, can you say this in the king's presence?" She replied, "Yes, my son." He said, "If that is so, when I go to the king today and ask you about your situation, please disclose this same information." Saying this, he went to see the king early, before court, and stood in the presence of the king. The queen also went there, and she, too, stood near the king.

Then the Enlightenment Being said, "Madam, you are very cruel. Would it not be good for you to give alms [*dāna*] in the name of your ancestors?" The queen said, "Oh child, I myself get nothing from the king. What can I give you?" He said, "Are you not the king's chief queen?" She said, "Oh child, when no respect is paid to the chief queen by the king, what can she do? And if the king does not pay respect to his queen, to whom will he pay respect? When we were on our way here and he had received a packet of food, the king gave me nothing, but ate it all himself." Then the Enlightenment Being asked the king, "Is that so, your lordship?" And the king indicated that it was so. When the Enlightenment Being saw the king agree with this, he said, "Then madam, why do you still live with the king? As the king does not love you, life here is full of pain for both you and for the king. Is such a life sufficient for you? If not, wouldn't you rather leave and live somewhere else, apart from him?" Hearing this, the king became afraid that his queen would leave him. The king then decided to give his kingdom to the queen, and the two of them lived together happily after that.

Saying this, the Buddha ended the Jātaka story of a packet of food.

"The couple at that time was the present husband and wife. And I, who am today the fully enlightened one, was the minister at that time."

The moral: "Married life is successful when a husband and wife share with one another."

The Story of a Crocodile
(Kumbhīla-Jātaka)

The master of all living beings told this story at the Bamboo Grove temple with regard to Devadatta.

Earlier, in the previously spoken *Kumbhīla-Jātaka*, this story was told except for two verses:[40]

"Hey monkey king, if someone can outdo your qualities
of truthfulness, good conduct, steadfastness, and generosity, then
he can overcome you.

"But these excellent good qualities that you have are
not shared by everyone. So they cannot overcome you."

The moral: "If someone is virtuous, he cannot be easily defeated."

---

40   See the *Vānarinda-Jātaka*, Jātaka No. 57 in Vol. 2 above. See also the *Suṁsu-māra-Jātaka* [No. 208].

A Story in Praise of Forbearance
(*Khantivaṇṇana-Jātaka*)

The omnipresent one who uniquely became a relative to the whole world, while he was living in Jetavanārāma, delivered this story about the king of Kosala.

This is how it was:[41]

At one time, there was a certain helpful minister of the king of Kosala who behaved inappropriately in the king's harem. The king overlooked this inappropriate behavior, and mentioned this to the Buddha. The Buddha then disclosed this earlier story:

At one time, when King Brahmadatta was ruling Benares, one of his close and helpful ministers engaged in wrongful behavior in the harem. In the meantime, a servant in the minister's home did likewise. [Thinking this was a good time to confess his own behavior to the king, about which he was feeling guilty], the minister took his servant to the king and complained, "Your lordship, this man, who is helpful to me, behaved wrongly in my home. What should I do?" Hearing this, the king said, "Hey minister, in my home also such a thing has been done by a faithful minister. You, too, should spread loving kindness upon him." Hearing these words, the minister said, "My lordship, I said this to you with my own behavior in mind, toward which your lordship has very graciously shown forbearance." And from that time on, the minister no longer behaved unwholesomely in the harem.

Saying this, the Buddha ended this story.

"The king at that time was I who have today become the Buddha."

---

41 The circumstances here are the same as in the *Pabbatūpatthara-Jātaka* [No. 195].

The moral: "When someone deserves punishment, it is best to do so with compassion so as to correct the bad behavior."

The Story of an Owl
(Kosiya-Jātaka)

When the omnipresent one who became the distinguishing mark [*tilaka*] of the whole world was living in Jetavanārāma, he disclosed this Jātaka story on account of the king of Kosala. The circumstances of its disclosure were given before.[42] The same is true here.

At one time, a certain king set out for war at an unseasonable time, and set up camp in his park. At that time, an owl flew into a thicket of bamboo and, hiding there, he slept. Some crows saw him, and they surrounded the thicket. The owl, waking up early, left when it was still daylight, which was an inappropriate time for him to set out. The crows that had surrounded the thicket saw the owl leave. And they attacked him, pecking at his head and causing him to fall to the ground. The king saw this and said to his minister, who was the Enlightenment Being, "Look at what is happening there."

The Enlightenment Being, who was his minister, said, "Your lordship, this owl came out of his hiding place at a time that was inappropriate for an owl, and because of this he came to a disastrous fate. If he had come out at night, he would not have faced such a danger." The king, hearing the Enlightenment Being's words said, "Yes, that is so." And he broke camp and returned to his palace.

Saying this, the Enlightenment Being ended this story of an owl.

"The king at that time was the Venerable Ānanda. And the minister was I who am today the Buddha."

The moral: "Everything has its season."

42   See the *Kalāyamuṭṭhi-Jātaka* [No. 176].

The Story of a Dung Beetle
(Gūthapāṇa-Jātaka)

Again, there was another story regarding a dung beetle delivered by the omnipresent one, who was like ambrosia to the world, while he was living in Jetavanārāma, on account of a certain monk. These are the circumstances of its telling:

There was a village known by many devout Buddhist householders that was between one and two *gāvuta*-s away from the city of Sāvatthi.[43] The villagers there used to offer alms to many monks on full moon days, half moon days, and new moon days. On other days, it was determined which monk would go for alms [*dāna*] to which house by means of a lottery system.[44] In this way, alms were constantly being offered to the monks.

At such times, there was a certain man who incessantly questioned the monks, bothering them in this way. Sometimes he would ask, "Why do we give *dāna* to you?" Other times, he would ask, "What have your thought processes gained by eating this food?"[45] When the monks could not answer his questions, he would preach to them. And in this way he humbled them. For this reason, many monks would not go there for alms.

In the meantime, a monk from a remote village came to Jetavanā-rāma. He asked the Jetavanārāma monks where he could go to gather

---

43 One *gāvuta* = a little less than two miles.
44 In order to avoid quarrels as to which monk should go for *dāna* to which house, tickets [*salākā*-s] fashioned from the rib of a coconut palm leaf were individually marked so as to indicate the homes of the various householders. Each monk would take one, and go to the respective home for *dāna* on that day.
45 When monks eat, they are supposed to reflect on twelve things, such as the impermanence of the food being eaten, and that the food eaten is done so to maintain one's strength.

alms [*piṇḍapāta*]. They told him about this village, and that in it there was plenty of alms but that there was there a man who bothered the monks by incessantly asking them questions. So it was better not to go there.

The visiting monk said, "Don't worry about that. If you can get me a lottery ticket, I will go there and I will handle this man in such a way that he will never again bother anyone." They said, "Alright. You can go today. We will give you one of the lottery tickets we have, that we decided not to use." He agreed, took the ticket, and went to the village.

When he got to the village's border, he tightly fastened his outer robe so that it would not fall off. The man who asked all the questions saw this, and he approached him like an attacking ram. He said, "I have a question. Before you go for alms, let me ask you my question." The monk said, "Layman, come with me to the village. I want to get some gruel first. After that, I will answer your question."

The monk then took the gruel, and went with the man to the village inn.[46] There, the man said, "Alright. Now you can answer my question." The monk said, "Please wait. Let me first drink the gruel and cleanse my teeth. After that, you can ask me your question." After that, the man said again, "Now, answer my question." And the monk said, "Let me clean up around where I have been sitting. After that, I will answer your question."

After he had cleaned up the place, the man said again, "Now, answer my question." Then the monk said, "The people who gave me this gruel are waiting to give me rice. Let me go there first, and bring back my bowl of rice. After that, I will answer your question. Take my bowl, and carry it for me."

The two went to the householder's home, and once there the monk received the rice. Then the monk gave the bowl with the rice back to the man, and told him to come with him to the outskirts of the village. Once there, he took the bowl of rice back from the man. The man again said, "Now, answer my question." The monk said, "Yes, I will answer your question now."

---

46   In the center of each village there was a shelter, or inn, where monks would gather to eat their food.

Saying this, he put down his bowl on the ground to the side, and without the man expecting it, he delivered a swift blow to the back of the man's head, causing him to fall to the ground. He then kicked some earth into the man's mouth and beat him. He then said, "For a long time, you have been bothering the monks who come to this village for alms. If you do it again, be warned!"

From that point on, when this man would see a monk, he would run away from him.

This story came to be known by the monks. One day, they were discussing it before the Buddha's evening Dhamma sermon. "Brothers, do you know the Bhikkhu [monk] so-and-so. That Bhikkhu kicked soil into the mouth of the man who would always question us monks in such-and-such a village." When the Buddha came there to preach the evening Dhamma sermon, he asked, "Oh monks, what were you talking about before I came here?" On hearing about what they were talking, the Buddha said, "Oh monks, not only now, but even in the past this Bhikkhu put dirt in that man's mouth." And he disclosed the past story. This is how it was:

At one time, long ago, the people of the kingdoms of Aṅga and Magadha were at peace with one another. Merchants from the two countries would travel back and forth between the two kingdoms. When they would come to the marshland beside the river that served as the border between the two kingdoms, they used to party, eating meat and drinking liquor.

At one time, there came a certain dung beetle who saw the leftover meat and alcohol. Drinking a little of the alcohol, he became intoxicated. When he then sat down on some of the nearby moist excrement and it gave way a little, he thought that the earth would not bear his weight. Thinking so, he became very proud.

In the meantime, there came a certain strong elephant who was in rut. Smelling excrement, he turned to leave. When the dung beetle saw this, thinking the elephant was afraid of him, he blurted out, "Hey, elephant king! Is someone as big as you turning away, afraid of a fight with someone who is as big as myself? Come and fight!"

The elephant heard this and turned back toward the dung beetle, saying to him, "What sort of a fight can there be between you and me? I do not want to even step on you with my clean foot, or attack you with my tusks. I do not want to even touch or hit you with my trunk. You are sitting on excretia. Therefore, I am going to treat you as the unworthy being you are by dropping dung on you."

Saying this, he dropped a piece of dung on him, and then after urinating on him, he trumpeted and went away.

The dung beetle died in that very spot.

In this way, the Buddha ended the story of a dung beetle.

"The dung beetle at that time was the man who would incessantly question the monks. The elephant was the monk who tamed the man. The forest deity who witnessed this event was I who have become the Buddha."

The moral: "A wise guy will always get his comeuppance."

The Story of the Brahmin Kāmanīta (or, Kāmanīya) [One Led by Desire]

(Kāmanīta-Jātaka, Kāmanīya-Jātaka)

When the Buddha who was like a storehouse of taste to the whole world was living in Jetavanārāma, he delivered this Jātaka story on account of the Brahmin named Kāmanīta. The circumstances of this are related in the twelfth book in the *Kāma-Jātaka* [No. 467].

[A Brahmin who dwelt in Sāvatthi started to cultivate a paddy field. When he was cutting down the trees to prepare the land, the Buddha was visiting Sāvatthi on his alms round. Passing there, the Buddha asked the man, "Oh Brahmin, what are you doing?" The Brahmin said, "Venerable sir, I am clearing the land to make a paddy field." The Buddha replied, "Very good."

The next day, when the Brahmin was burning the cut down trees, the Buddha passed the same way. He saw the Brahmin and asked, "Oh Brahmin, what are you doing?" The Brahmin said, "Venerable Gotama, I am burning the cut down trees." The Buddha replied, "Very good." Saying this, he went away.

On the day the Brahmin was making embankments for watering the field, the Buddha passed by again the same way. The Buddha stopped off to the side of the road again, and asked the Brahmin, "Oh Brahmin, what are you doing?" The Brahmin said, "Venerable Gotama, I am making embankments so as to provide the field with water." The Buddha replied, "Very good." And he went away.

On the day the Brahmin was sowing the field with rice, the Buddha passed the same way. He said, "Oh Brahmin, what are you doing?" The

Brahmin said, "Venerable Gotama, I am sowing the rice." The Buddha replied, "Very good." And he went away.

And when the paddy was full grown, the Buddha passed the same way and asked, "Oh Brahmin, what are you doing?" The Brahmin said, "Venerable Gotama, I am viewing the ripening paddy." Saying this, the Brahmin thought he would give the Buddha and his monks alms when the plants were harvested.

As the Brahmin had been seeing the Buddha constantly from the time he started to prepare the field for planting until now, he had a feeling of intimacy with the Buddha. And that night, the Brahmin went to bed thinking that the next day he would harvest the rice and give the Buddha and his monks the alms.

That night, a torrential rain occurred in the upper reaches of the Aciravatī River, and a flood washed away all the plants in the field, not leaving even a single stalk. In the morning, when the Brahmin got up and went to see the field, he did not see any paddy. Everything had been washed away to the ocean. The Brahmin, not seeing the paddy, started to cry loudly and beat his chest. He became overwhelmed with grief.

With his divine wisdom, the omnipresent one saw this Brahmin who had become overwhelmed with grief and thought, "I will go and release him from his grieving." He summoned a newly ordained monk, and he went with him to the Brahmin's home. The Brahmin saw the omnipresent one and said, "Venerable Gotama, I have had a great loss. If I am correct, you came to see me to console me in my grief." And he prepared a seat for the Buddha to sit down.

The omnipresent one said, "Oh Brahmin, why have you become so overwhelmed with grief?" The Brahmin said, "Venerable Gotama, you visited with me from the time I started to prepare my field for cultivation. You have seen how I have toiled to bring my field to the point of being ripe for harvest. Last night, this field that was now ripe for harvest was washed away by the flood from the Aciravatī River without leaving even a single stalk of rice. If this had not happened, I would have been able to fill up 1,000 cartloads of paddy. And I was thinking of giving alms to the Buddha and his entire community. But all my efforts and intentions have come to nothing. It is because of this that I am grieving."

The omnipresent one on this occasion said, "Let go of something that has gone. You ought not have remorse." Saying this, the Buddha stated the discourse of the *Kāma Sutta* and preached to him.[47] And the Brahmin, listening to that discourse attained the path leading to the stream entrance state of mind [*sotāpattimagga*], which is endowed with a thousand means of attainment.

On that day, the monks who were assembled in the preaching hall in the evening to listen to the Buddha's Dhamma sermon were discussing the deep grief of this Brahmin and how the Buddha had pacified it. While the monks were discussing this, the Buddha entered and sat down on the prepared seat. He said, "Oh monks, what were you discussing before I came here?" The monks told him about what they were discussing. The omnipresent one said, "Oh monks, it is not only today, but even in the past I have calmed this Brahmin's mind." And the monks invited the Buddha to disclose the past story.]

When King Brahmadatta was ruling Benares, his nephew went to rule in a country in which Brahmadatta had declined the throne. The nephew ruled this country with greed, hatred, and stupidity. The god Sakka saw that he was ruling this country with greed, and decided to deceive him. Thinking so, he disguised himself as a young Brahmin, went to the king, and said, "Your lordship, I have seen the three cities that are known as Northern Pañcāla, Indapatta, and Keka (or Kekaka; also Kekaya).[48] These three kingdoms can easily be conquered by us with just a small army. They are heavily endowed with plenty of pearls, jewelry of all kinds, conches, and various gems and coral, as well as with many other valuable stones. Seeing them, I came to tell you that they are vulnerable. If you wish, we

47   See *Suttanipāta*, verses 766-71 [=IV.1.1-6].
48   In ancient times, these were considered to be the chief three cities of Jambudīpa, or India of the Buddha's time. Indapatta is the modern city of Delhi.

can easily conquer them tomorrow. Without delay, organize your fourfold army tomorrow morning as we ought to leave as soon as possible."

The king heard this, and he became very happy. He said to the young Brahmin, "Come here, directly to me, tomorrow early in the morning."

And the god Sakka who was disguised as this young Brahmin went away to his home.

The next morning, the king prepared his fourfold army and asked his ministers, "Where is the young Brahmin who came yesterday with the promise of our conquering three kingdoms?" The ministers said, "Your lordship, we did not provide him with food and lodging, or other necessities. Did you make arrangements for him?" The king said, "No, I did nothing. Go around the city and look for him." They said, "Yes, your lordship." And they went throughout the city, but they could not find him. The king became very upset, thinking that the young Brahmin had gone to another country as he had not prepared proper lodging for him. Thinking this, he became very upset that he had lost the expected wealth from the three cities. Because of grieving about this, he got very sick and among other ailments, he began to have diarrhea. Many physicians came there to treat the king, but they could not cure him.

Sakka saw this and decided to go to the king, release him from his grief, cure him of his ailments, and free his craving mind of greed. He came to the palace gate disguised as a Brahmin and said, "There has come a physician who knows how to cure the king's diarrhea." The king, hearing this news, thought, "Even the most highly qualified physicians have not been able to cure me. How will such a man do it?" Thinking this, he said, "Give something to him, and let him go."

Hearing that, the god Sakka said, "I did not come to earn a fee. I came to the palace to cure the king." Hearing these words, the king said, "If so, then let him come." Sakka came to the king and said, "Your lordship, the diarrhea is due to blood and bile. It comes to people because of fear and grief. How did this sickness come about? If you tell me that, then I can cure you."

The king heard these words and said, "Oh Brahmin, a young Brahmin came to me and said that he would be able to obtain for me the states of Northern Pañcāla, Indapatta, and Kekaya. I failed to entertain him. I think that because of this he went away to another kingdom. On account of the grief from thinking so, that because of my failure to entertain him I lost a great gain, I came down with this sickness."

Hearing these words, Sakka said, "Your lordship, once annexing those three states to your present state, would you be able to wear four sets of robes at the same time? While ruling the four states, would you be able to eat food from four plates at the same time? Would you be able to sleep on four beds at the same time? If you go on a journey, could you travel by four vehicles at the same time? You could not do so. [You can only enjoy one at a time.] As this is so, now you can better understand the cause of the pain you have suffered on account of craving such an over-expanded state. You can understand that there is on these accounts no reason for you to crave for the three cities that you have lost. To cure your sickness, there is no physician throughout all of Jambudīpa other than myself."

The king said, "Yes, good physician. Your reasoning is very good. By whatever stratagem you know, please heal my sickness, removing from me my grief."

Then, the king of the gods Sakka said, "Yes, your lordship. I can do that." Saying this, he advised the king, "Your lordship, craving, anger, delusion, and like unwholesome thoughts, are all looked down upon by wise people. Such thoughts lead to unhealthy and loathsome situations. Those thoughts pave the way for suffering in awful hells." Saying this, he instructed the king on the badness of unwholesome thoughts, instilling in him the fear of such awful re-becomings. Pointing out to him the sufferings in such awful states, he made the king become afraid of craving.

In this way, Sakka made the king afraid of craving, anger, and delusion. And he channeled his mind toward the value of controlling such unwholesome thoughts. Sakka advised the king to develop wholesome thoughts in order to keep his mind clear of such unwholesomeness. And he further instructed the king to rule his country according to the ten righteous practices of kingship [*dasarājadhamma*]. By practicing them conscientiously, without violating them, he might even be able to become the next king of the gods.

The king, hearing the words of the Brahmin physician, who was the king of the gods, gave up his craving for the lost three kingdoms. Simultaneously, his sickness disappeared from his mind and body. And Sakka returned to his divine world.

The king ruled his country practicing righteousness and with devout thoughts from that time on. He lived long, and finally passed away.

Saying this, the revered Buddha ended the story of the Brahmin Kāmanīta.

"The king at that time is today the Brahmin Kāmanīta. And I who am today the Buddha was then Sakka, the king of the gods."

The moral: "Worldly things are impermanent. One ought to not grieve over them."

The Story of Running Away
(The Story of the Mendicant Palāsa)
[One Who Thinks in a Bad and Conceited Way]
(Palāyi-Jātaka, Palāsa-Jātaka)

The Buddha, who was the cause of people's achieving *nibbāna* [release from re-becoming], delivered this Jātaka story while he was living in Jetavanārāma. These are the circumstances of its delivery:

At one time, there was an ascetic named Palāsa who came to the city of Sāvatthi lording the challenge, "There is no other ascetic in all of Jambudīpa who can win an argument with me." At that time, the Buddha who could challenge every argument was living in Sāvatthi. The citizens said, "Even were there a hundred mendicants like you, none would be able to challenge the Buddha's arguments."

Hearing these words, the mendicant said, "If so, I would like to engage in a dispute with the Buddha Gotama." Saying this, he went surrounded by many people to see the Buddha. When he saw the seventh outer gateway [*dvārakoṭṭhaka*] of Jetavanārāma,⁴⁹ he asked, "Is this the perfumed chamber of the omnipresent Gotama?" The people said, "Oh mendicant, this is not the perfumed chamber. This is only the seventh outer gateway. Buddha's chamber is splendid like Vejayanta palace [of the god Sakka]." On hearing these words, the mendicant thought, "If the seventh outer gateway is like this, what would the dwelling itself be like?" Imagining this, he became afraid of going to argue with the omnipresent one, and he went away.

---

49   There were seven concentric fences around Jetavanārāma. This is the gateway of the outermost one.

The crowd of people that had gathered shouted out triumphantly, and went to see the Buddha. The Buddha, on seeing them, asked, "Oh laymen, why have you come at this unusual time?" Hearing the news about the mendicant from the people, the omnipresent one said, "Not only today, but even in the past this mendicant, on seeing the outer gateway of my dwelling, has fled." The people then requested that the Buddha relate the story. The Buddha did so. This is how it was:

At one time, the Enlightenment Being was ruling in the city of Takkasilā in the kingdom of Gandhāra. At that time, King Brahmadatta of Benares went to Takkasilā to conquer it with his fourfold army. He said to his army, "Let my elephants that are in a threefold rut[50] and are on account of this capable of fighting enemy elephants go to the various gates and fight all elephants that come out of them. In the same way, let my armored horses go to the various gates and fight all horses that come out of them. Let my decorated chariots go to the various gates and fight all chariots that come out of them. Let my foot soldiers go to the various gates and fight all foot soldiers that come out of them. Let everyone in the fourfold army with bows and arrows shoot them, causing a rain of arrows. Those who have swords, let them strike with them in every which way." Ordering his army like this, he came to the seventh gateway of the city of Takkasilā.[51] Seeing its magnificence, he asked whether this was the gateway of the palace. His soldiers said, "No. This is not the palace's gateway but the city's seventh gateway." Hearing this, the king became afraid of fighting, thinking that if the seventh gateway of the city is like

---

50   When a male elephant is in rut, a liquid comes out of the elephant's two cheek folds and penis, the intoxicating smell of which is attractive to female elephants. Such elephants are more aggressive, and will fight readily with other male elephants.

51   Ancient cities had around them seven concentric moats symbolizing the seven oceans encircling Mount Meru and the mountain ranges around it. Evidence of such moats can be seen even today around Yangon (Rangoon). Each of these moats had over them a gateway at each of the city's four directions. King Brahmadatta has here come to one of the four outermost gateways of the city of Takkasilā.

this, how mighty would be the palace gate. Imagining such a mighty palace, he turned and fled away with his army.

Saying this, the omnipresent one ended this Jātaka story.

"The king of Benares at that time was the mendicant known as Palāsa. And I who am today the Buddha was the king of Gandhāra who dwelt in the city of Takkasilā."

The moral: "People are fooled by their conceit."

The Second Story of Running Away
(The Second Story of the Mendicant Palāsa)
(Dutiya-Palāyi-Jātaka, Dutiya-Palāsa-Jātaka)

Again, when the noble omnipresent one was living in the Jeta Grove temple in Sāvatthi, this Jātaka story was disclosed. These are the circumstances of its disclosure:

A certain mendicant called Palāsa once came to dispute with the omnipresent one surrounded by a large number of people. Arriving at the preaching hall in Jetavanārāma, he saw the Buddha's beautiful looking face shining with splendor and brilliance. He thought, "I may not be able to win an argument with such a glorious person." And he became afraid of engaging in a dispute with the Buddha. Becoming afraid of the Buddha in this way, he ran away without saying anything to the crowd of people that had accompanied him. The crowd of people, when they saw this, became filled with joy of the Buddha's nature and shouted out the triumph. They then stayed to listen to the Buddha preach, none of them following any longer the mendicant Palāsa.

The omnipresent one addressing all the people who were present said, "Oh laymen, not only now, but even in the past this person has been defeated merely on seeing my face." The people present then asked the Buddha to disclose the past story. The Buddha disclosed it in this way:

At one time, there was a king ruling in Benares called Brahmadatta, who was the Enlightenment Being. At that time, the king of Takkasilā surrounded by his fourfold army came to conquer the kingdom of Benares. As the king of Gandhāra was just about to storm the city of Benares, seeing his army, he said, "The power of my army is so great that it can be seen by its hoisted banners alone. Seeing these, one can only imagine that the king of Benares will flee at their sight. Just as a bird is not able to cross over the great ocean, just as a huge rock cannot be shaken by a ball of cotton yarn, none will be able to conquer me and my fourfold army."

Hearing these words, the king of Benares standing on the watchtower of the city gate, said to the king of Gandhāra, "Fool, what is the purpose of such a useless boast? You may in fact not be able to defeat my army with yours."

Hearing these words of the king of Benares, and seeing his face which was beautiful and splendid like a full moon, he feared that he would indeed not be able to conquer such a powerful king. And he turned back to his own country.

"The king of Gandhāra at that time was the mendicant Palāsa. The king of Benares was I who have attained enlightenment."

The moral: "Conceit leads to defeat."

The Story of a Sandal
(*Upāhana-Jātaka*)

On another occasion, when the omnipresent one who became the universal monarch of the doctrine [*dhamma*] was living in the Bamboo Grove temple, this story was disclosed with regard to Devadatta.

One day, the monks who were assembled in the preaching hall were discussing about the monk Devadatta. They said, "Monk Devadatta has done many wrongs to his master, the omnipresent one. As a result of those bad deeds, he has fallen into disaster." While they were discussing this matter in this way, the omnipresent one came into the preaching hall. He asked, "Oh monks, what were you talking about before I came?" The monks told him about what they were talking. When the Buddha heard this, he said, "Not only now, but even in the past, Venerable Devadatta learned from me and after, being conceited and thinking that he was my equal, he came to disaster." The monks then invited the omnipresent one to disclose the past story. The Buddha did so:

At one time in the past, a king called Brahmadatta was ruling the city of Benares. At that time, the Enlightenment Being was born into a family of mahouts.

Once, a certain young man from the kingdom of Kāsi came to the city of Benares and asked the Enlightenment Being to teach him the art of being a mahout. The Enlightenment Being taught him his skills, as much as he knew them, without hiding anything from him. This young man, when he understood that he had learned all that the teacher had to offer, said to his master, "Respectable master, please take me to the king so that I may serve him."

The teacher, who was the Enlightenment Being, agreed to this. But first, he went to the king alone and said to him, "Your lordship, I have a student who would like to serve you. So, if you wish, you may take him into your service, paying him whatever you want." The king, hearing this news, said, "If that is so, I will pay him half of what I pay you. Tell him that he may come and serve me for that payment."

The teacher returned home and said to his student that the king had agreed to take him into his service for payment of half of what he, the teacher, received. Hearing these words, the student said, "Why, master, is this so? I have learned everything that you know. If he pays you a certain amount, why should not I also receive the same amount? Why should I only receive half?" And the Enlightenment Being went back and told this to the king. Then the king said, "That is O.K. You may both receive the same stipend, provided he shows that he has the same skills as you do." The Enlightenment Being told this to his student, and the student agreed to compete against his master.

When the king heard this news, he had an announcement made throughout the city that the king's mahout would compete with his student the next morning in a display of their skills.

Then, the Enlightenment Being thought, "If I am to compete with him, I must use a stratagem." That night, he trained an elephant to do everything in reverse. When he ordered it to go, it would stop. When he ordered it to stop, it would go. When he ordered it to lie down, it would get up. And when he ordered it to get up, it would lie down. When he ordered it to give something, he trained it not to give. And when he ordered it not to give something, he trained it to give.[52] In this way, in one night he trained the elephant to do everything in reverse.

The next morning, the Enlightenment Being mounting that elephant, went to the king's palace yard for the competition. Many people were gathered there. His student also came, mounted on an

---

52   According to Sri Lankan elephant trainers, there are a total of 15 commands
     that they use to train elephants.

elephant. The people gathered there were eager to see the competition between the two mahouts.

When the Enlightenment Being ordered his elephant to go forward, it went backward. When he ordered it to go slowly, it ran forward fast. When he ordered it to stand, it lay down. When he asked it to lie down, it stood up. When he asked it to take something, it let it be. When it was asked to let something be, it picked it up. The student did not know how to match this.

Seeing this failure, the people gathered started to abuse the student. They shouted, "Hey wicked student, you are competing against your teacher. You do not know your own measure. You are thinking that you are your teacher's equal. But it is not so." Some of them took clubs and stones, and they beat him to death.

The Enlightenment Being, dismounting his elephant, approached the king and said, "Your lordship, when an art is acquired by an ignoble person, it will lead to disaster, just as a wrongly made sandal bought [for a cheap price] in the street, in the summer cuts the wearer's foot, wounding it and thereby leading to distress. In the same way, when a person of low status [*nīca*] learns a noble art, it leads to his own undoing. When a worthy person [*sappurisa*] studies an art, it will lead to benefit for both himself and others." Hearing these words of the Enlightenment Being, the king became very pleased. He gave the Enlightenment Being many gifts, and conferred on him honors showing his appreciation.

Saying this, the Buddha ended the story of a sandal.

"At that time, Devadatta was the student. And I who am today the Buddha was the master mahout."

The moral: "Parents and teachers always have knowledge learned from experience, which their children and students do not have."

The Story of the Curved Body of a Lute [The Story of One with a Stick of Bamboo as a Support]

(*Vīṇāthūṇa-Jātaka, Veṇuthūṇa-Jātaka*)

Again, once when the omnipresent one was living in Jetavanārāma temple, the Buddha delivered this Jātaka story on account of a certain young girl who was the daughter of a millionaire. These are the circumstances of its delivery:

There was living in Benares the daughter of a millionaire. At the home of the millionaire, there was a very large bull that was very much respected as a deity by the household. The young girl one day questioned one of the household's slave girls, saying, "We have many bulls at our home, but this one is respected more than all the others. What is the reason for this?" The slave girl replied, "Can you not see that this bull has a very huge hump on its back. Because of this, we respect him as the king of our bulls."

One day, this millionaire's daughter saw a man walking on the street who was a hunchback. She thought, "If my household considers worthy of worship a bull because it has a big hump on its back, this man also must be worthy of worship." Thinking so, she thought further, "I was born in a respectable family. This man must be of an even more worthy family." On this account, she decided to go and live with him. She took with her a young slave girl from the household, and slipping out a side door of the mansion, she went away with the hunchback.

These events became known even among the community of monks. One evening, when the monks were gathered in the preaching hall to listen to the Buddha's sermon, they were talking about this. When the omnipresent one entered, he asked, "Oh monks, what were you talking about before I came here." They told him about what they were talking. The Buddha said, "Oh monks, not only now, but also in the past in a previous life, this young girl became attached to this same man and did a similar thing." The monks then asked the Buddha to tell the past story. And the Buddha, assenting to their invitation, told the past story.

One time, when a king called Brahmadatta was ruling the city of Benares, the Enlightenment Being was born in a millionaire's family in a remote village. He had many sons and daughters. At the same time, there was another millionaire in the city of Benares. It was arranged that the latter millionaire's daughter would marry one of the Enlightenment Being's sons. The latter millionaire also owned a bull that was very much revered by the family on account of its large size. That millionaire's daughter one day asked one of the household's slave girls, "Why does my family revere this bull?" The slave girl said, "This bull is not like the other bulls. Other bulls are smaller. And this bull has a larger hump on its back than other bulls. Because of this, this bull is a king of bulls. So we honor him and revere him more that the other bulls."

On hearing these words, that millionaire's daughter thought, "If this is so, then hunchbacks must be revered as kings among men." One day, this girl saw a hunchbacked man in the street. She thought, "As this man has a very large hump on his back, he must be a very noble person. So, I ought to be with such a person." Thinking this, she summoned one of the household's slave girls and asked her to tell the hunchback to wait at such-and-such a place until she was able to come. The hunchbacked man did so. The millionaire's daughter, taking with her some valuables from her home, disguised herself, slipped out a side door, and went to join the hunchback. While they were walking on the road, the hunchback became overcome with pain, and he lay down on the side of the road curled up in a ball. And the young girl sat down by his side.

At that time, the Enlightenment Being was traveling the same road, going to the city of Benares to fetch the young girl to be his son's wife. Seeing the couple, he stopped to talk to them, and he realized that this was the same young girl he was going to Benares to fetch. Talking to the young girl, he understood that she had run away from home by her own decision. He asked the millionaire's daughter, "Why did you run off with this hunchback, having been born in such a noble family?" The millionaire's daughter said, "At our home, our family members revere our largest bull with a big hump on its back. For that reason, I thought that this man with a hump on his back would also be worthy of great respect. So I decided to go away with him."

The Enlightenment Being, hearing these words, understood what had happened. He took the girl into his chariot and brought her back to her mansion, where he had her wash her hair and bathe.[53] He then took her again in his chariot, and brought her back to his home where she wed his son.

Saying this, the omnipresent one ended this Jātaka story of one with the [curved] body of a lute.

"The millionaire's daughter at that time was the same as the millionaire's daughter today. And the millionaire in the remote village was I who am today the Buddha."

The moral: "Simple minded people do simple minded things."

---

53   Such was done for ritual cleansing.

233

The Story of a Harpoon
(*Vikaṇṇava-Jātaka*)

When the omnipresent one who became a gift to the world guiding the way out of re-becoming was living in Jetavanārāma, he told this Jātaka story about a monk who was infatuated with a woman. The circumstances of its delivery are as follows:

There was a certain monk who was infatuated with a woman. On this account, he was dissatisfied with his monkhood in the Buddha's dispensation. On hearing about this, the Buddha said, "This monk, even before on account of his cravings, was similarly killed by a very sharp barbed harpoon. Just as before, he will die in this life by the piercing barbed arrow of his cravings." The monks present then asked the omnipresent one to disclose the past story. And the Buddha then told the story.

This is how it was:

One time in the past, the Enlightenment Being was born as the king of Benares known as Brahmadatta. One day, he came to enjoy himself on the lake in his pleasure garden. He got into the large boat that was there with dancers, musicians, and singers, and as he was enjoying himself on the lake, he saw that the boat was being followed by many fish. On seeing all the fish, the king asked one of his ministers, "Why are these fish following us?" The minister said, "They are following us to offer you their services." Then the king said, "In that case, they deserve to received from us some support." Thinking this, he ordered a minister to daily give them a measurement of rice to eat.

The minister did so each day. But whenever he gave them rice to eat, a certain crocodile also came. So the fish were afraid to come to eat. The minister told this to the king, and told him that because of this, not all the rice was being eaten. The king told the minister to take a sharp barbed harpoon, and to kill the crocodile with it. In accord with the king's order, the minister got on a boat in the lake, and following the crocodile when it came to eat, he pierced him through and through with the sharp barbed harpoon. Seeing the wounded crocodile, the minister said, "Hey crocodile, you will die because of your cravings." And full of pain, the crocodile went back to his dwelling place, and died there.

The omnipresent one said, "Oh monks, anyone who falls into craving, will die on account of their cravings as did this crocodile, losing the object of their cravings."

The omnipresent one disclosed this teaching, and after that he expressed the four noble truths. After he had expressed the four noble truths, the monk who had become distressed with his monkhood attained the stream entrance state of mind.

The Buddha then ended this Jātaka story.

"At that time, I who am today the Buddha was the king of Benares."

The moral: "The cravings of sensual desires bring danger."

The Story of Asitābhū (Ahitābhū)
[One Who Turns Herself Towards Non-Attachment]
(Asitābhū-Jātaka, Ahitābhū-Jātaka)

The omnipresent one who was a big river of noble teachings [dhamma] delivered this story while he was dwelling in Jetavanārāma with regard to a certain young girl who left her husband shortly after she was married.

Once, there was a young girl who was given in marriage to a young man of a nearby village. The young man who married her had no attachment to this girl, and wandered the streets here and there seeking enjoyments. The young girl also had no care about her marriage. As her family was close to the Buddha's two chief disciples, she used to regularly offer them alms [dāna] both at home and at the temple, and would listen to their sermons and advice. She attained the stream entrance state of mind because of this, and she decided to become a nun. She got permission to be ordained from her parents and she became a nun, entering the convent. There, through meditation, she developed intuitive knowledge of life [vipassanā] and became a saint [Arahant].

This story became known among the monks. They talked about it appreciatively one evening when they were assembled in the preaching hall. When the Buddha came there, he asked them, "Oh monks, what were you talking about before I came here?" They told him about this girl, saying that by entering the convent, she had freed herself from the cycle of re-becoming [saṃsāra]. The Buddha said, "Oh monks, not only today, but even in the past she relieved herself from her burden of lay life, turning toward a higher state." The monks then asked the omnipresent one to disclose the past story.

This is how it was:

At one time, there was a king called Brahmadatta in the city of Benares. The Enlightenment Being was at that time born into a Brahmin family. After he had become educated, he renounced lay life and went to the Himalayan forest where he ordained himself as an ascetic. Through the cultivation of meditation, he developed mental absorption [*jhāna*]. And he remained there, living in the forest.

At the same time, the king of Benares had a grown son. This son took his wife, named Asitābhū, and went to live in the Himalayan forest. There, he settled near the Enlightenment Being's hermitage. Once, he saw a beautiful female Kinnara[54] passing near his dwelling, and he became infatuated with her. Having no regard for Asitābhū, he chased after this female Kinnara.

His wife thought, "Being faithful to my husband, this young prince, I came to the forest with him, giving up the luxuries of the palace. This being so, why does my husband now chase after this bird? I do not want to live with him anymore." And she went to the nearby ascetic, who was the Enlightenment Being, and said, "Respectable one, I would like to be ordained as an ascetic. Please give me the ordination as an ascetic." The Enlightenment Being ordained her. There, in his hermitage, she devoted herself energetically toward meditation and gained miraculous powers [the *abhiññā*-s]. Through association with the Enlightenment Being, she gained these miraculous powers and the eightfold powers of concentration [*aṭṭhasamāpatti*].

When the young prince was unable to catch the female Kinnara, he returned to his dwelling. Not finding his wife there, he went to the Enlightenment Being's hermitage. There he saw his young wife.

---

54   The most popular conception of a Kinnara is that it is a being with the body of a bird and the head of a human. There are other ways of imaging Kinnara-s as well.

The young wife said, "Your lordship, you left me alone, chasing after a female Kinnara. Because of that, I have been lucky enough to obtain a high state of mental absorption. Therefore, I can no longer remain with you in marriage." She thanked him for his infidelity, and through her miraculous power, she rose up into the sky and went away.

The young prince became very unhappy and said, "If a man craves too much, he will face many difficulties. I have seen this now for myself, now that my wife Asitābhū has left me."

After a time, the young prince heard that his father was dead, and went back to the city of Benares to become king.

In this way, the Buddha ended this Jātaka story of Asitābhū.

"The young wife at that time was this nun. And the young prince was this householder. The ascetic was I who am today the Buddha."

The moral: "Sometimes, what seems to be misfortune, is good fortune in disguise."

(235)

The Story of Vacchanakha
(*Vacchanakha-Jātaka*)

While the omnipresent one who was like a universal monarch to the noble doctrine [*dhamma*] was living in Veḷuvanārāma, he delivered this Jātaka story with regard to the Venerable Ānanda.

The Venerable Ānanda had a friend called Roja, who was a wrestler. He sent a message to the Venerable Ānanda that he would like to see him. The Venerable Ānanda told the Buddha, and got his permission to leave. He then went to see his friend at his friend's home. Roja served Venerable Ānanda delicious food for lunch, and after he said to Ānanda, "Dear friend, why do you remain in the robe? Why do you not leave monkhood, and come to live with me here?" I have many pearls, gems, and a great deal of wealth. Why should we both not enjoy them together?" Saying this, he emphasized the value of the life of a householder. The Venerable Ānanda, hearing this, told him the negative side of the life of a householder. He emphasized the beneficial results of monkhood, and returned to Veḷuvanārāma.

When the omnipresent one heard this news, he said, "In the past, also, the wrestler Roja spoke in the same way." The monks present asked the Buddha to disclose the past story. And the Buddha disclosed it.

This is how it was:

At one time, a king named Brahmadatta was ruling in the city of Benares. At that time, the Enlightenment Being was born into a Brahmin family. Renouncing lay life, he went to dwell in the Himalayan forest. Once, he returned to the city of Benares to get some salt and sours.

The millionaire of Benares saw him, and was pleased with his demeanor. He invited him to come to lunch at this home. After, the Enlightenment Being dwelled there for a time, and the two developed a close friendship. The millionaire thought that he would like to get this ascetic, Vacchanakha, to disrobe and to become a householder dwelling together with him in his mansion, the two of them enjoying together the fivefold sensual desires. One day he gave him lunch, and after he said, "Revered ascetic, Vacchanakha, why do you live the humble life of an ascetic? It is full of misery. It would be better if you were to become a householder and enjoy with me the fivefold sensual desires." Hearing this, the Enlightenment Being said, "The fivefold sensual desires only seem to be happiness to those who are unwise. But they are, in fact, just a fetter. It is better to give up such suffering, and to live in the forest eating fruit and yams." Saying this, he left the millionaire's mansion and returned to the Himalayan forest.

In this way, the Buddha ended this Jātaka story of Vacchanakha.

"The millionaire at that time was the wrestler Roja. And I who am today the one who has become enlightened was then the ascetic Vacchanakha."

The moral: "The pitfalls of lay life are not a temptation to those who are wise."

The Story of a Crane
(Baka-Jātaka)

This Jātaka story was delivered while the omnipresent one, who is similar to a great ocean, was living in Jetavanārāma on account of a monk who was a hypocrite. These are the circumstances of its delivery:

A certain monk who was a hypocrite re-stitched and cleaned an old robe and brought it to Jetavanārāma. Some monks at Jetavanārāma saw the robe, which appeared to be very beautiful, and they all asked him to give it to them. He said, "Oh, I got this robe only through great effort. How can I just give it to you?" One of the monks said to him, "If that is the case, let me give you in its stead another robe." The monk who lived a hypocritical way of life agreed to this, and received from the other monk a new robe. The monk who received the re-stitched robe later discerned that it was really a ragged old ordinary cotton robe. Realizing this, he brought the hypocritical deceiving monk to the Buddha, and complained about what this monk had done. On seeing him, the Buddha said, "Oh monks, not only today has this monk engaged in hypocrisy, but he did so also in previous lives." The monks then asked the Buddha to disclose a story of olden times. And the Buddha disclosed it in this way:

At one time, when King Brahmadatta was ruling the kingdom of Benares, the Enlightenment Being was born as a fish. He became the king of many fish.

A certain crane once came to the lake where these fish lived. Thinking he would deceive the fish, he stood still in the water with his wings spread, his neck bent, with his glance toward the water, pretending to be an ascetic engaged in asceticism. While he was standing still like this, the fish who was the Enlightenment Being came near him with the other fish. When they came near to him, the other fish looked at him admiringly as if he were a white lotus, saying, "This must be a very virtuous ascetic."[55] The Enlightenment Being, hearing this, said, "Hey fish, this is no ascetic. He is looking for an opportunity to seize you. There is no virtue in him. He is just a killer."

The fish then understood the truth of what their king said, and they splashed water, driving away the crane.

Saying this, the omnipresent one ended this Jātaka story about a crane.

"The crane at that time was this hypocritical monk. And the king of the fish was I who am today the Buddha."

The moral: "A clever person can plot to deceive, but he does not foresee the consequences of his deception once the deception is uncovered."

---

55   White is considered to represent purity.

237

The Story of Sāketa
(*Sāketa-Jātaka*)

This Jātaka story was previously spoken in the first book under the name *Sāketa-Jātaka* [No. 68].

When the Buddha was living in the city of Sāketa, at one time a Brahmin named Sāketa addressed the Buddha as if he were a loving relative of the Buddha's. The circumstances of this were given in the previous *Sāketa-Jātaka*.

The Buddha was born in a previous life as a son to this Brahmin. The monks asked, "Venerable sir, can past attitude toward a person [*vāsana*] continue into a future life?"

The omnipresent one responded, "Oh monks, just as a dried-out lotus takes life anew once put again in water and mud, so also the sentiments of former associations come back again in later lives when one meets a person again or when one gains again possession of anything. This Brahmin couple were my parents in many births. And I who am today the Buddha has been their son many times."

Saying this, the Buddha ended the story.

The moral: "Meritorious love never dies."

The Story of a Single Word
(Ekapada-Jātaka)

When the omnipresent one who became the crown of the world was living in Jetavanārāma, he disclosed this Jātaka story with regard to a certain householder. These are the circumstances of its delivery:

A certain householder who lived in Sāvatthi was playing with his young son, who was sitting on his lap. The son said to the father, "Oh my father, tell me about the mansion that has only a single door [ekadvārapāsāda] but many rooms circling it on the inside." The father thought, "I do not know the answer to this question. But the Buddha has omnipresent understanding. He will know the answer." Thinking this, he took his son with him to the Buddha, paid respect to the Buddha, and said, "Revered one, my son here asked me a question about a mansion with a single door. I do not know how to answer him. If your reverence can explain it to us, it would be a great blessing."

The Buddha said, "Oh householder, this young boy asked this question even before, and wise people explained it to him many times in the past. But as it is concealed along with his former births, he does not remember it now." Invited by the householder to disclose the old story, the Buddha did so.

This is how it was:

At one time, King Brahmadatta was ruling the kingdom of Benares. The Enlightenment Being was born at that time in a millionaire's family. One day, the great being was sitting with one of his sons on his left. The son said, "Father, can you tell me the one word that covers everything, that is known [to all] as the single door [ekadvāra]?" The great being said, "Oh my son, there is no advantage in speaking many words. If one maintains just one precept, non-injury [*ahiṁsā*], it forestalls many defilements and the killings of many living beings." Saying this, the Enlightenment Being disclosed the meaning of the single door [*ekadvāra*].

"The son at that time is this boy today. And the millionaire of Benares was I who am today the Buddha who has attained enlightenment."

At the end of this teaching of the law [*dhamma*], both the father and the son attained the stream entrance state of mind, which can be reached by a thousand paths.

The moral: "When a person develops a desire for truth, it remains with them always."

Further,

"Following the precept of not harming others [*ahiṁsā*] prevents many unwholesome thoughts and defilements, and stops many killings."

The Story of a Green Uncle[56]
(Haritamāta-Jātaka)

When the omnipresent one who was like a distinguishing mark on the forehead [tilaka] to the world was living in the Bamboo Grove temple [Veḷuvanārāma], this Jātaka story was delivered with regard to King Ajātasattu.

The younger sister of the king of Kosala, King Pasenadi, was married off to King Bimbisāra. At that time, the king of Kosala's father, Mahā-Kosala, gave his daughter a village to use the revenue from for bath money. Later, King Bimbisāra was killed by his son, Ajātasattu. And his queen, being very saddened by his death, died out of grief.

The king of Kosala was angered, and said, "I will not allow that village to be kept by a rogue who killed his father." Because of this, the two of them, uncle and nephew, fought continuously. On some occasions, King Pasenadi was defeated and went home dejected. On other occasions, King Ajātasattu was defeated and went home dejected.

When King Ajātasattu won the battle, he marched back to his capital city triumphantly with pomp. When he was defeated, he snuck back silently, not letting anyone know of his return.

One day, the monks who were assembled in the preaching hall to hear the Buddha's evening sermon, were talking about this matter. When the omnipresent one entered, he asked, "Oh monks, what were you talking about before I came here?" The monks told him about what they were talking. Hearing this, the Buddha said, "Oh monks, not only today, but

---

56 *Māta* literally refers to a mother's brother. It is used here to indicate respect for a person. In this case, it refers to the green frog who is the Enlightenment Being in the Jātaka story.

even in the past Ajātasattu behaved like this." The monks then asked the Buddha to tell the story of old. And the Buddha disclosed the past story.

At one time, when King Brahmadatta was ruling the kingdom of Benares, the Enlightenment Being was born as a big green frog in a certain lake. At that time, a fisherman came there and set out a net to catch fish. Many fish were caught in the net. Meanwhile, a certain water snake also entered the net, thinking this would be a way to get easy prey. But many large fish came up to the snake and bit off pieces of him, causing him to bleed. The water became red with his blood. Through his wile, the snake slipped out of the net. At that moment, the green frog came near the net. Seeing him, the snake said, "Hey green frog, do you see the way these fish have treated me? Is this a proper way for them to behave?" And the green frog said, "They are doing to you, in their territory, what you would do to them in your territory." While they were talking like this fish, seeing that the snake was weakened, came out from the net and came up to him, and bit him to death.

In this way, the Buddha ended the story of a green uncle.

"The water snake at that time was King Ajātasattu. The green frog was I who am today the fully enlightened one."

The moral: "As you do to others, they will do to you."

The Story of the First King Piṅgala
[One with Dark Red Eyes]
(Mahāpiṅgala-Jātaka)

When the omnipresent one who was like a banner of the Law [dhamma] was living in Jetavanārāma, he delivered this story with regard to Devadatta. These are the circumstances of its narration:

The Venerable Devadatta was sick for nine months. Finally, he decided to come to see the Buddha, and he came toward Jetavanārāma. Before he reached Jetavanārāma, he fell off the stretcher on which he was being carried by four monks and fell onto the ground, which opened up and swallowed him. In this way, he fell into hell. Many divine beings, Brahmā beings, and human beings, on seeing this or on hearing about this, became filled with joy because of it.

One day, the monks assembled in the preaching hall for the Buddha's evening sermon, were talking about this fruition of Devadatta's deeds [kamma]. When the Buddha entered, he was told that the monks were talking about this. The Buddha said, "Oh monks, not only today, but even before in the ocean of re-becoming [saṃsāra], a multitude of beings rejoiced on Devadatta's death." The monks asked the Buddha to disclose the old story. Then the Buddha disclosed the old story hidden by time in this way:

At one time, there was a king called Piṅgala ruling in the city of Benares. He was very cruel to his subjects, imposing on them many punishments and insults without any reason. He heavily taxed his subjects, squeezing the wealth out of them. He had no mercy, even on his sons, friends, relatives, ministers, and soldiers, just as he had none on the householders in his kingdom. Everyone thought of him as a thorn stuck in his or her own body, and they all hated the king, wishing to show him no mercy or kindness.

The Enlightenment Being was born to King Piṅgala as his son. The king reigned a long time, and finally he died. On his death, many people became very happy. They brought hundreds of cartloads of firewood, and with anger made a huge pyre. They then quenched the funeral pyre with hundreds of jugs of water that they brought. Immediately, they held a coronation ceremony for his son, who was the Enlightenment Being. Thousands of householders and ascetics rejoiced that they finally had a righteous king instead of that old unrighteous king. At that time, though, one of the old king's doorkeepers started to cry without being able to stop.

Seeing this doorkeeper, the Enlightenment Being said, "My father crushed the juice out of people as if they were sugarcane in a press. Because of this, people called him Piṅgala [Red-Eyed].[57] Now that he is dead, everyone is rejoicing. While they are rejoicing, you are crying without stopping. What goodness was done to you by my father?"

The doorkeeper, hearing this, said, "I am not crying because of any goodness your father showed me. Whenever he used to go upstairs or downstairs, he would hit me eight times on my head with his fist. As this is his practice, when he goes to hell, he will hit the gatekeeper there the same way. And the people in hell, seeing this, will send him back here. Then, he will hit me again in the same way. It is because of this, that I am crying."

The Enlightenment Being thought, "I will have to comfort this poor man." He said, "My father was burned by hundreds of cartloads of firewood. And the kindled pyre was doused with hundreds of jugs of water. Around that area, a high wall was erected. Such a dead person will not come back into this world in the same form again. Therefore, do not worry!" In this way, he comforted the man.

---

57   When one exerts too great an effort at something, one squeezes his eyes closed shut causing them to become red. Red eyes are considered in South Asian culture to be ugly, and to be an indication of an ugly nature.

"King Piṅgala at that time was the monk Devadatta. And the righteous king who was the son of King Piṅgala was I who have today become Buddha, the fully enlightened one."

The moral: "No one grieves for an evil person."

The Story of Sabbadāṭha
[Chief of All Toothed Creatures]
(*Sabbadāṭha-Jātaka*)

W hen the omnipresent one who was a treasure of teachings was living in Jetavanārāma, he delivered this Jātaka story with regard to Devadatta. These are the circumstances of its delivery:

One day, the monks assembled in the evening in the preaching hall were talking about how Devadatta had lost both reputation and gain of livelihood on account of the incident involving the elephant Nālāgiri.[58] When the Buddha entered the preaching hall, he asked, "Oh monks, what were you talking about before I came here?" The monks told him about their discussion. Hearing this, the omnipresent one said, "Oh monks, not only today, but even in the past Devadatta similarly lost his gain and fame." And the monks requested the Buddha to tell them the old story.

This is how it was:

At one time, when King Brahmadatta was ruling the kingdom of Benares, the Enlightenment Being was the king's chief advisor. The Enlightenment Being had mastered the three Veda-s and the 18 branches of knowledge [*sippa*-s], and knew a certain spell known as the *Pathavijaya Manta*, 'The Spell to Conquer the World.' This spell had the power of bringing all creatures under one's control. Because of this, the Enlightenment Being would not recite it [for the purpose of renewing his memory of it] in earshot of others, lest they learn it. One day, he was reciting this spell in a lonely spot outdoors while sitting on a slab of stone.

---

58 At Devadatta's instigation, the elephant Nālāgiri, when drunk, was let loose for the purpose of trampling the Buddha while the Buddha was on his alms round. But Nālāgiri became tame in the Buddha's presence, and paid him reverence instead.

At that time, a certain jackal who happened to be hiding under the slab of stone heard the Enlightenment Being recite it, and learned it by heart. The reason he was able to learn it so easily, is that in a previous life he had been a Brahmin who knew this spell. On this account, he learned it at once. When the Enlightenment Being was leaving that lonely spot, saying that he had now refreshed his memory enough, the jackal also came out of hiding, saying mockingly to the Enlightenment Being, "I, too, have now learned it enough!"

Hearing these words, the Enlightenment Being became afraid. He thought, "Because of this jackal, many people will be killed." And he chased after the jackal, calling out, "Catch that jackal!" But the jackal ran faster than him, and hid in the forest. In the forest, he saw a she-jackal. He said to her, "Do you not know who I am?" The she-jackal asked, "Why does your lordship ask me that?" Then the jackal said, "Do you not recognize me? I am the king of all four-footed creatures." And he recited the spell in her presence. At that time, many jackals came around him, surrounding him.

Then lions, leopards, elephants, horses, tigers, bear, deer, antelope, as well as boars, hares, and such other animals came and surrounded him. The jackal then made the she-jackal his consort. And he named himself Sabbadāṭhaka, 'The Chief of All Toothed Creatures.' He declared himself as their king. And he thought, "I would like not only to be king of animals, but also the king of all humans." Thinking this, he summoned two elephants, had a lion placed on their backs, and on the back of the lion, he sat with his queen. With all the animals surrounding him, he went toward Benares and surrounded the city, his host covering an area of twelve Yojana-s all around the city. He then sent a message to the king, saying, "Give me your kingdom, or wage a war!"

The citizens of Benares, seeing all the wild animals such as lions, and so forth, surrounding the city, became very afraid. They closed the city's gates and their houses' doors, locking them all shut, and they stayed inside.

The Enlightenment Being, hearing this news, approached the king and said, "Your lordship, do not be afraid of this jackal, Sabbadāṭhaka. Let the war against Sabbadāṭhaka be my responsibility." Saying this, he climbed up one of the gate towers and called out to Sabbadāṭhaka, "Hey jackal, how do you plan to wage your war against the city of Benares?" Then the jackal said, "I will have my entire community of jackals howl. And by their howling, I will make the citizens of Benares afraid. Then the citizens will flee, and I will take your city."

On hearing this, the Enlightenment Being said, "Hey jackal, how will you take the city if all the citizens do not flee?" And the jackal said, "I have an army of lions. They will roar. And hearing their roaring, the rest of the citizens will be afraid and will flee. Then, for sure, I will be able to take your city."

On hearing these words, the Enlightenment Being came down from the tower. He then had a proclamation made, that all citizens should stuff their ears with chickpea flour, as well as the ears of cats, pet birds, and so forth. When the citizens had done this, the Enlightenment Being again climbed up into the gate tower and called again to the jackal. He asked, "Hey jackal, do you think that high-born lions will roar at the request of a menial creature like yourself?"

The conceited jackal, hearing these words, said, "Hey Brahmin, not only will all the other lions obey me, but even will this lion on whose back I sit." And the Enlightenment Being said, "If that is so, ask them to roar." And the jackal gave a sign to roar, to the lion on whose back he was sitting. Then the lion, annoyed, bit the head of one of the elephants and roared at the jackal. And the two elephants became afraid on account of the roaring noise. They started to run away, and the jackal fell to the ground under their feet and was trampled to death. Further, all the rest of the elephants, hearing all the lions roaring and having no space in which to run, fought with one another to be able to get space to flee first and trampled all the other running creatures to death at the spot. The citizens of Benares, seeing all the creatures running, took the chickpea flour out of their ears and out of the ears of all their pets. Then they saw all the dead animals around the city.

The Enlightenment Being came down from the gate tower upon seeing all the dead animals around the city. Then he had proclaimed that all the citizens should take the chickpea flour out of their ears, and that they should gather up as much meat as they desired. The citizens ate all the fresh meat that they could, and the rest of it they dried and preserved. According to tradition, it is from this time that people first started to make dry meat.

In this way, the omnipresent one ended this story of Sabbadāṭha.

He then added further, "Oh monks, this jackal, Sabbadāṭhaka, failed to maintain the kingship that was easy for him to come by, and fell into disaster on account of his conceit. In the same way, when someone gains wealth, if he becomes conceited, he also will lose everything and perish.

"The jackal Sabbadāṭhaka was Devadatta. The king of Benares was the Venerable Sāriputta. And the Brahmin advisor was I who have become the Buddha."

And the omnipresent one ended this Jātaka story of Sabbadāṭha.

The moral: "It is not good to become conceited on account of gain, or depressed when faced with loss."

The Story of a Creature That Has Good Nails
(*Sunakha-Jātaka*)

When the omnipresent one who was a bridge across the ocean of re-becoming [*saṃsāra*] was living in Veḷuvanārāma, he told this story about a dog that used to be fed in the reception hall for visiting monks, called Ambalakoṭṭhaka.

The people who used to bring the water to the reception hall, brought a little puppy there. They asked the monks to let it live there and eat the monks' leftover rice. The dog was given much rice by the monks. And he grew up to be a very big dog.

One time, a man who came from far away saw this dog there. He gave the people who brought the water to the reception hall a small sum of money and a piece of cloth for the dog, tied him to a leather leash, and led him away. The dog, not barking or resisting, followed his new master and ate whatever he was given to eat. He behaved as if the man had always been his master.

The man who had taken the dog thought, "The dog is faithful to me." Thinking this, he released him from the leash. The dog immediately ran away, and returned to the place from where he had been taken.

This incident was spoken about by the monks who were assembled in the preaching hall for the evening Dhamma sermon. When the Buddha entered, he asked, "Oh monks, what were you talking about before I came here?" The monks told him about what had happened regarding the dog. The Buddha said, "Oh monks, not only today, but even in the past this dog knew how to deceive people." The monks then asked the Buddha to disclose the old story. And the omnipresent one then disclosed it.

This is how it was:

At one time, King Brahmadatta was ruling Benares. A certain householder brought up a little puppy. He gave that little puppy a lot of food to eat. And by eating that food, the little puppy grew up to be a very fat dog. A certain man from a remote village saw this dog. Being interested in buying the dog, he gave the householder a thousand gold coins and a piece of fine cloth. Tying the dog to a piece of rope, he took the dog. The dog went with him without barking or resisting in any way. The dog behaved as if the man was known to him. Whatever he was given to eat, he ate. When they had reached the middle of the forest, the man was tired. So he tied up the dog to the stump of a tree by the roadside where a number of people were resting, and there he lay down to sleep.

At that time, the Enlightenment Being was passing by that place and saw the dog. He said, "A dog can gnaw through a piece of rope and free himself, so as to return home. Yet you do not do this. How foolish you are!" The dog responded, "Wise man, you are right. What you have said occurred to me as well. If I do not do that, he will keep me even longer and take me even further away to his home. I am waiting for an appropriate moment when everyone is fast asleep." Saying this, when everyone was in deep sleep, the dog gnawed through the rope and returned to his earlier master's home.

In this way, the teacher of the whole world ended the story.

"The dog at that time was the same dog as today. And the wise man was I who have become the Buddha."

The moral: "Even dogs are faithful to those they love."

The Story of [the Musician] Guttila[59]
(Guttila-Jātaka)

When the omnipresent one who became a ship over the ocean of re-becoming [saṁsāra] was living in Veḷuvanārāma, he delivered this Jātaka story with regard to the Venerable Devadatta. These are the circumstances of its delivery:

One day, an assembled community of monks said to the Venerable Devadatta, "Brother Devadatta, you learned the whole Tipiṭaka from the Buddha. You attained the fourth mental absorption [jhāna] on account of the Buddha.[60] This being so, the omnipresent one having helped you like that in so many ways, why do you now think you are your teacher's equal? And why do you now oppose him?"

Hearing this, Devadatta said, "Brothers, what has the omnipresent one done for me? Everything I gained was on account of my own good fortune. It was I, myself, who learned the Tipiṭaka. I, myself, attained the fourth mental absorption. How has the omnipresent one helped me?"

This was being talked about one day by the monks in the preaching hall. When the omnipresent one entered, he asked, "Oh monks, what were you talking about before I came here?" The monks told him about what they were talking. Then the omnipresent one said, "Oh monks, it is not only now, but even before, in the past, Devadatta repudiated his teacher." The monks asked the Buddha to disclose the old story. And the omnipresent one disclosed the story to them.

---

59 This Jātaka story was made the subject of a famous medieval Sinhala poem, and on this account has become the subject of much discussion in Sri Lanka. Compare the story here to that of the Upāhana-Jātaka [No. 231] above.

60 When one obtains the fourth mental absorption, he is then able to obtain miraculous powers, such as the power of levitation, and divine eye.

This is how it was:

At one time, a king called Brahmadatta was ruling Benares. At that time, the Enlightenment Being was born in a family of musicians. When he grew up, he learned all subjects regarding music and became well-known throughout Jambudīpa as Guttila the Musician. He never married, and he maintained his blind parents on his own.

Once, a group of merchants came from Benares to the city of Ujjain. One day, they wanted to enjoy themselves by bathing and feasting. And they wanted to hear music. So they asked for a musician to be brought. A musician known by everyone, who was the chief musician in Ujjain, was brought. He was known as Mūsila the Musician. He played and danced his best for them. But the merchants were not satisfied. So the musician Mūsila played again for them in a lower key. But, again, they were not pleased even a little. Finally, he played for them in the highest key he could. But no one enjoyed the music. The musician Mūsila thought, "These people do not know anything about music. So, let me play for them as if I am playing for someone who knows nothing about music." Even then, no one showed any appreciation.

Then Mūsila asked them, "Why do you not show any appreciation while I am playing for you, even when I play my best in both high key and low key? Are you too ignorant to like my playing? Have you ever seen a musician better than me?"

Hearing these words, the merchants said, "Oh musician Mūsila, to us who have heard the music of Guttila the Musician in Benares, your playing sounded like a bow being pulled along a piece of bamboo." Then Mūsila the Musician said, "If that is so, take me along with you when you return to Benares." They agreed, and when they went back to Benares, they took Mūsila the Musician with them and showed him the house of Guttila the Musician. Showing him this, they went back to their own houses.

The musician Mūsila went to Guttila the Musician's house. At that time, the Enlightenment Being was not at home. Mūsila saw the Enlightenment Being's lute [vīṇā], and he took it and started to play.

Hearing that sound, the Enlightenment Being's blind parents said, "It sounds like our son's lute is being gnawed by mice." At once, Mūsila got up and paid respect to the Enlightenment Being's parents, seeing them. He asked, "Where has your son gone?" The Enlightenment Being's parents said, "He will return at any moment. Please be seated." At that very same moment, the Enlightenment Being returned.

Mūsila the Musician saw the Enlightenment Being and asked him to teach him his musical art. The Enlightenment Being, who was able to read people's features and understood their character, could see that Mūsila was not a good man. He said, "No, I will not teach you music. Please go away."

Even though the Enlightenment Being did not want to teach him music, Mūsila requested him to do so through his parents again and again, asking his parents to please have their son teach him music. And he won over the minds of the Enlightenment Being's parents. As the Enlightenment Being could not refuse his parents, he agreed. He taught him all he knew, without keeping anything back.

When the Enlightenment Being went to see the king, he was in the habit of going accompanied by his students. When the king asked him who this man was, the Enlightenment Being responded, "He is my student." Mūsila was introduced to the king in this way. In the course of time, the king came to trust Mūsila. At last, the Enlightenment Being said, "Son, you now know all that I know."

One day, Mūsila thought, "It would be good to get a good job now. Rather than going to a remote city, let me stay and get a job here in Benares. My teacher is now old. Let me stay here." Thinking this, he said to his teacher, "Revered teacher, I would like to serve the king. Please tell him, and ask him to set a wage for my livelihood." The Enlightenment Being went to the king and said, "Your lordship, my student would like to serve you. Please set a wage for him." The king said, "Good. I will give your student half of what you get as his wage." The Enlightenment Being went home and said to his student that he would be given as his wage half of what the Enlightenment Being gets. The student said, "Why should I get only half of what you get, when I know all that you know?" The teacher told this to the king. The king said, "If he can show that he knows as much as you know, then his wage will be the same."

The Enlightenment Being told this to his student. And the student agreed to this condition. The king summoned the Enlightenment Being and his student. In the presence of both of them, the king asked, "Hey, Mūsila! Are you willing to engage in a contest with your teacher, Guttila?" Mūsila said, "Yes, your lordship. I am willing to compete with him. Do not I know everything that he knows? On the seventh day from today, we can compete."

The king declared that the great musician Guttila and his student Mūsila would compete after seven days in the palace courtyard. The Enlightenment Being thought, "This competition will be between a young man and an old man. He has the strength of youth, whereas I am old and no longer have such energy. Because of this, I may well be defeated. But even if I win, I am defeated, since there is no great credit if my pupil is beaten. Therefore, let me not be defeated by him in either way. It would be better to die in the woods." Thinking this, every day he would go to the woods out of fear of shame, and then changing his mind from fear of death, he would return. By the seventh day, the grass on his path was trampled under, and it had become a footpath.

On the seventh day, after he had gone into the woods, the granite throne of Sakka, the king of the gods, became warm. The king of gods then investigated, using his divine eye, to see who was trying to take his throne through force. He saw the Enlightenment Being in his confusion and he went to him and asked, "Why, Venerable master, are you here in the woods?" Then the Enlightenment Being asked, "Who are you, sir?" He said, "I am the god Sakka, the head of the twofold divine world."[61] The Enlightenment Being said, "Your lordship, tomorrow there is supposed to

61　The twofold divine world is comprised of the Caturmahārājika [the lowest of the six devaloka-s, or worlds of divine beings, which includes the human world] and the Tāvatiṁsadevaloka [the second devaloka, the world of the 33 Vedic gods].

be a competition between myself and my student as to who plays better the seven-stringed lute. Your lordship, god Sakka, who was born in the Kosiya clan, please assist me."[62]

The god Sakka said, "Yes, Venerable master, I will help you. Go and play just as well as he does. Then, as I give you signs, one by one break each of the seven strings, while continuing playing on your lute. As each string breaks, it will continue to sound. He, too, will then break his strings one by one, but he will no longer be able to play. Then, throw up into the air these three dice, one by one. 900 divine damsels will come there and dance. And I, too, will appear then to everyone." Saying this, the god Sakka disappeared.

Many people heard the news that the next day there would be a competition between the musician Guttila and his student Mūsila. Around the courtyard they set up seats, tier above tier. Other people came by chariots, and sat on the roofs of their chariots.

The Enlightenment Being took his usual lute and also came to the courtyard and sat on a seat that had been prepared for him. Mūsila also sat on his own seat. People watched, as did also the king. The god Sakka was also there, invisible, in the sky. Only the Enlightenment Being could see the god Sakka. Then, the Enlightenment Being started to play. Mūsila played the same piece. Everyone appreciated the playing of the two musicians. Then the god Sakka gave the Enlightenment Being the sign to break the first string. From the broken string, there came divine sound more beautiful than before. Mūsila, seeing that, also broke a string. But from it, there came no sound. In this way, the Enlightenment Being broke all seven strings one by one. And celestial sound continued to come from each of them. Mūsila did the same. But from the strings of his lute, there came no sound at all. The Enlightenment Being started to play on the handle of the lute. And the sound spread through all of Benares city. When Mūsila did the same, there came no sound. And it was as if he were fingering a piece of bamboo.

---

62 The Kosiya clan is a Brahmin clan that is noted for voluntarily helping others.

At that moment, the Enlightenment Being threw up into the air one of the three dice that had been given him by the god Sakka. 300 divine damsels appeared and started to dance. He threw up the second die, and there came another 300 dancing damsels. When he threw up the third die, still another 300 dancing damsels appeared. In this way, 900 divine damsels appeared. In the meantime, the Enlightenment Being was playing on the lute music that was in his thought. Seeing this miracle, the king and the many citizens of Benares rejoiced in Guttila's music. And with Mūsila, the king was displeased. He looked at his ministers' faces, and the ministers understood the king's intentions. They took their walking sticks and clubs, and hit Mūsila, saying that he had gone against his own teacher. And they threw him out of the city.

The king was very pleased with the Enlightenment Being. He gave him much gold and many jewels. And the crowd of people threw on him jewelry as if it were a sudden torrential rain. The king of the gods said to the Enlightenment Being, "Tomorrow, I will send to your home my chariot, Vejayanta. Get on it, and come to see me." Saying this, he went to the divine world.

The damsels in the divine world asked, "Oh lord Sakka, where have you gone? You were not here." Sakka said, "I went to listen to the lute playing of the musician Guttila." These divine damsels said, "Your lordship, we also would like to listen to the lute playing of Guttila." The next day, the god Sakka sent his divine vehicle Vejayanta with Mātali, his charioteer, to Guttila's home.

The Enlightenment Being took his lute and got into the chariot. He came in it to the god Sakka. The god Sakka asked him to play the lute. The Enlightenment Being said, "Your lordship, musicians do not play their music without being paid. So, if I play, what will you give me?" Sakka said, "If you play, I will give you much wealth." When he said this, the Enlightenment Being said, "Your lordship, I do not need any wealth. I would like to hear the previous merit of your 32 divine damsels that brought them to this world. That is enough for me as my pay." The divine damsels said, "Oh Venerable master, we will disclose to you all our previous meritorious deeds. But first play."

The Enlightenment Being agreed, and began to play his music. He played as if he were a divine musician.

After doing so, he asked the first divine damsel whose body was shining as if she were the evening star, "What sort of meritorious deed did you do to get such a beautiful body and such a large retinue?" She said, "Oh musician, when I was in the human world, I gave a couple of white cloths to an Arahant who had been ordained in the community of the Buddha Kassapa, the fully enlightened one. As a result of that good action, I was born in the divine world with such splendor."

Then the Enlightenment Being questioned the others as well. The others also explained to him their meritorious actions. This is how it was:

One said, "I was born in the divine world by offering a bunch of flowers to a Buddha." Another one said, "I offered perfume at a shrine [*stūpa*]. Because of this, I was born in the divine world." Others said, "We were born in the divine world by offering fragrant objects at shrines." Still another one said, "I was born in this divine world by offering sweet fruit to monks." Some others said, "We also were born in this divine world by giving sweet fruit to monks." Another one said, "I offered five-scented perfume at a shrine of the Buddha Kassapa."[63] Still another said, "I gave food to and listened to the preaching of a monk who had lost his way, and I directed him as to how to get to where he wanted to go." Another said, "I was born in this divine world because I gave alms to a monk." Another one said that she was born in the divine world as a result of giving water to a thirsty monk who was sailing on a ship. Another one said that though constantly insulted by her aunt and uncle, she offered them only loving kindness. Because of this, she was born in the divine world. One said that she was born in the divine world because of the meritorious action

---

63 Five-scented perfume is composed of *kunkuma* [saffron], *yavanapuppha* [the *yavana* flower], *turukkatela* [the oil of the *turukka* plant], *tagara* [Sinh. *tuvarala*; the fragrant powder of the *tagara* plant, *Tabernaemontana coronaria*], and *candana* [sandalwood].

of giving her share of food to other hungry people, eating only a small portion of rice. Another one said that she had been born as a slave, and had given whatever she received in compensation to others.

In this way, all 32 divine damsels explained the meritorious actions that they had done that resulted in their being born in the divine world.

The Enlightenment Being enjoyed hearing all this very much, and said, "I have now received the results of my good deeds in the human world."

He returned to the human world and disclosed these stories to many people in the world. In this way, he persuaded them to do good actions.

Hearing him, many people did good actions.

In this way, the Buddha ended this Jātaka story of Guttila.

"The musician Mūsila at that time was Devadatta. The king of Benares was the Venerable Ānanda. The god Sakka was the Venerable Anuruddha. The musician Guttila was I who am today the Buddha."

The moral: "Even though a noble person may not always receive just gratitude for his actions, he will receive plentiful rewards."

$$\boxed{244}$$

The Story of Desiring Too Much[64]
(Vīticcha-Jātaka)

When the omnipresent one who crossed over the ocean of re-becoming [saṁsāra] was living in Jetavanārāma, he delivered this Jātaka story with regard to the wanderer Palāsa.[65] These are the circumstances of its delivery:

The wanderer Palāsa thought that throughout the whole of Jambudīpa, there was no one who could best him in an argument. When he came to the city of Sāvatthi, he said to the populace, "There is no one who can argue with me and win." Then the people said, "Someone like you ought to meet the Buddha and then argue with him. Go to the omnipresent one." He agreed to go. And together with a crowd, he went to see the Buddha at Jetavanārāma. There he argued with the Buddha.

The omnipresent one said, "Sir, I have answered all your questions. Now, let me ask you just one question. What is the meaning of 'one'?" Palāsa did not understand the meaning of this. So he was defeated and ran away.

Many elderly monks assembled in the preaching hall in the evening talked about this incident. When the omnipresent one came to the preaching hall, he asked, "Oh monks, what were you talking about before I came here?" The monks told him about what they were talking. The Buddha then said, "Oh monks, not only today, but even in the past, he was defeated by me with a single question." The monks asked the Buddha to disclose the story of the past. The Buddha then disclosed this story:

---

64   When a monk is seeking alms, a civil way of refusing to offer such a gift is to say, "aticchatha (bhante)," or "Desire more [than I can give you], sir," implying "Please go on, sir." Pāli vīti is a contracted prepositional combination of vi + ati, representing an intensified ati.

65   Compare Jātaka-s No. 229 and No. 230 above, which are also about Palāsa.

At one time there was a king called Brahmadatta in the city of Benares. At that time, the Enlightenment Being was born as a Brahmin. Seeing the disadvantages of enjoying the five sensual desires, he renounced lay life and went to dwell in the Himalayan forest. There, he ordained himself as an ascetic and he practiced asceticism.

In the meantime, a certain mendicant came to a village near where the Enlightenment Being was dwelling. This mendicant said to the villagers, "There is no one who can beat me in an argument." The villagers said, "In the forest, there is an ascetic who is eloquent. He can beat you in an argument." Saying this, they took him to the Enlightenment Being. Many people went along to witness this.

The Enlightenment Being welcomed everyone and said, "Please drink water that I have brought from the river nearby, and quench your thirst." Then the mendicant, who was his guest, thought, "This is a good chance to start an argument, picking on his first words." He said, "What is the river? The near bank, or the far bank, or the water in the middle? Which of these three do we refer to as the river?" Then the Enlightenment Being said, "If the far bank is not the river, and the near bank is not the river, and the middle of the water is not the river, where, then, would the river be?" Then the guest mendicant thought, "By picking on my argument, he has defeated me. How can I argue with him now?" Thinking this, he felt shamed and he fled.

In this way, the Buddha ended this Jātaka story of desiring too much.

"The mendicant at that time was this wanderer Palāsa. And the ascetic was I who have become the fully enlightened one."

The moral: "Do not bite off more than you can swallow."

The Story of the Succession of Causes
(*Mūlapariyāya-Jātaka*)

When the omnipresent one who helped people who enjoyed the temporary happiness of the ocean of re-becoming [*saṁsāra*] was living in Jetavanārāma, he delivered this Jātaka story with regard to 500 Brahmin monks. These are the circumstances of its delivery:

500 Brahmins who were well versed in the *Tipiṭaka* of the Buddha were very conceited. Being conceited, they used to say, "We also know the whole *Tipiṭaka*, just as the Buddha." Because of their conceit, they ceased waiting on the Buddha. This came to be known by the Buddha. The Buddha, knowing this through his divine eye, when he was dwelling in the park in Subhaga woods, near the city of Ukkaṭṭhā, summoned them and preached the discourse [*sutta*] known as 'The Succession of Causes.'[66]

This was discussed one evening in Jetavanārāma by the monks assembled in the preaching hall. When the Buddha went there, he asked, "Oh monks, what were you talking about before I came here?" The monks said that they were discussing the way in which the Buddha removed the conceit of the 500 Brahmin monks. The Buddha said, "Oh monks, not only today, but even in the past I have humbled them and broken them of their false pride and conceit." Then the monks said, "Venerable sir, you know this story clearly, but we do not. Please tell us." In this way, they requested the Buddha to disclose the story of the past. The Buddha then disclosed the story.

---

66 This is the first *sutta* of the *Majjhimanikāya*. In this, the Buddha explains various contemporary systems of philosophy and points out the differences between them and his own system. It also deals with the theory of the non-existence of a soul and Nibbāna.

At one time, King Brahmadatta was ruling the city of Benares. At that time, the Enlightenment Being was born as a Brahmin teacher. He taught 500 Brahmin youths as his students. He taught them energetically, and they became well versed in the three Veda-s.

After the completion of their studies, these youngsters became very conceited, thinking that they knew all that their teacher knew. Being conceited in this way, they became very proud and no longer came to assist their teacher. The teacher understood this situation.

One day, when the teacher was near a certain jujube tree that had fallen down in the garden, the students saw him and so as to mock him, they tapped on the tree and said, "This tree has no hard core." The teacher understood that they were referring to him. In order to show them their foolishness, he crafted a riddle for them to solve in a certain stanza:

"Time consumes all, even itself.

But who can consume the all-consumer?"

The answer to this riddle is than an Arahant, one who has destroyed the thirst of the sensual desires and so lives as not to be born again, is one who consumes time. The teacher, speaking this stanza, gave the students seven days to solve the riddle. The students agreed to this. But on the seventh day, they could not give the meaning of the stanza. Then the teacher said, "You all have big heads, but they are like the nuts of the palmyra tree.[67] You think that I know nothing and that you know more than me, but you know nothing. You do not even know the meaning of this stanza." Saying this, he ridiculed their behavior. Then the students understood the weakness of their knowledge and begged the pardon of their teacher.

Saying this, the Buddha ended the Jātaka story of the succession of causes.

---

67   The nut of the palmyra tree contains much fiber, but very little water and three very small rough kernels.

"The students at that time were the Brahmin monks. And the teacher was I who am today the fully enlightened one."

The moral: "An empty container makes the biggest sound."

The Story of Advice Regarding Food Cooked with Oil [The Story of Advice to a Fool]
(*Telovāda-Jātaka, Bālovāda-Jātaka*)[68]

When the omnipresent one, the lord who crossed over the ocean of re-becoming [*saṁsāra*], was living in the temple called Koṭāgāra in the city of Vesāli, he delivered this story on account of General Sīha. These are the circumstances of its delivery:

The omnipresent one preached to General Sīha, and he attained the stream entrance state of mind. From that day, he used to invite the Buddha to lunch. He prepared the lunches with various types of meat and fish. The omnipresent one, together with many disciples, accepted this food.[69]

This was observed by the Jain master Nigaṇṭhanāthaputta who, however, was not sure whether or not the Buddha ate this food that was offered to him. He was under the impression, though, that this food was prepared especially for the Buddha and his community. So, he accused the Buddha of eating such food with meat prepared especially for him.

One evening, the monks gathered in the preaching hall in the evening were talking about this accusation. When the Buddha came

---

68   The Sinhalese manuscripts here read *Telovāda-Jātaka*. The Burmese and Thai manuscripts give the title as *Bālovāda-Jātaka*. See the footnote to this story in Ven. Pandit Widurupola Piyatissa Mahā Nāyaka Thera's edition of Buddhaghosa's commentary. The generally adopted edition of the Pāli text in the West, that of V. Fausbøll, adopts here the reading of his Sinhalese manuscripts.

69   General Sīha, as he had attained the stream entrance state of mind, wanted to offer *dāna* [alms] to the Buddha and his community. Therefore, he prepared for them lunches just as he would prepare these for himself. When one offers *dāna*, it is customary to give one's own usual fare.

there, he asked them, "Oh monks, what were you talking about before I came here?" The monks said, "Bhante, Niganthanāthaputta has blamed you for eating left over food that had meat in it." Then the Buddha said, "Yes, monks, Niganthanāthaputta blamed me for this in a previous life also." The monks asked the Buddha, "Venerable sir, we do not know of that. Please disclose to us the past story."

This is how it was:

At one time, King Brahmadatta was ruling the kingdom of Benares. At that time, the Enlightenment Being was born as a Brahmin. When he grew up, he became an ascetic and lived in the forest. Once, he came to the city of Benares in search of salt and sours.

A certain householder in Benares saw the Enlightenment Being going on his alms round. Seeing him, he made up his mind to try to shake the Enlightenment Being's religiosity. He invited him to his home for lunch, and entertained him with tasty food. After the meal, he said to the ascetic, "Revered one, for the sake of your food, I have killed many living beings, hurting them. If I have received any demerit from killing those innocent beings in order to give you this meat, that demerit is to be shared by us half and half."

Then the Enlightenment Being said, "If you were to have killed your wife and children, and given me their flesh to eat, I would have had to eat it out of loving kindness and compassion."

Saying this, the Enlightenment Being got up and left for the Himalayan forest.

In this way, the Buddha ended the Jātaka story of 'Advice Regarding Food Cooked with Oil.'

"The householder at that time is today Niganthanāthaputta. And the ascetic was I who am today the Buddha who has attained full enlightenment."

The moral: "There is no fault in eating whatever food is offered to one as a guest."

$$\boxed{247}$$

The Story of the Prince Pādañjali
[One Who (Mistakenly) Holds Two Feet Together in a Gesture of Offering][70]
(Pādañjali-Jātaka)

*A*gain, when the enlightened one who released countless people from the ocean of re-becoming [saṁsāra] was living in Jetavanārāma, he disclosed this story with regard to the Venerable Lāḷudāyi. The circumstances of its delivery are as follows:

One day, the Venerable Sāriputta and Moggallāna, the Buddha's two chief disciples, were answering the other monks' questions regarding Dhamma [doctrine] in the preaching hall. Those monks were very pleased with the answers given by the two chief disciples, and took great pleasure in their solutions to the various problems. While the monks were enjoying the discussion, the Venerable Lāḷudāyi came to the preaching hall. He said to the assembled monks, "The two chief disciples have said what I already know." Hearing these disruptive words of Lāḷudāyi, the two chief disciples went away.

When the Buddha heard this, he said, "Oh monks, not only today, but even in the past this monk Lāḷudāyi, rather than say anything sensible, just made a meaningless sound with his lips." The monks said, "Venerable sir, tell us how it was." In this way, the Buddha was invited by them to disclose the past story. The omnipresent one then related this story.

At one time, King Brahmadatta was ruling in the city of Benares. At that time, the Enlightenment Being had become an advisor to the king

---

70 It is normally two hands that are held together in a gesture of offering. To mistakenly hold two feet together in such a gesture is the mark of a fool.

who organized all his affairs. The king had a son called Pādañjali. In time, the king died suddenly. All his ministers organized the king's cremation. After the king's cremation, the ministers decided to consecrate the king's son, Pādañjali, as the new king. Deciding this, they wanted to examine his knowledge to see whether or not he would be able to carry on the affairs of the kingdom. Thinking so, they related a certain incident which was bad, and said it was good. They then asked the prince his opinion about that.

The prince made his lips quiver, and said nothing. The ministers thought the prince had understood their question, but that they had not understood what he said.

On the second day, when they asked the prince another question, he again just made his lips quiver in the same way. This time, the ministers understood that the prince did not know how to answer their question. The ministers understood that he knew nothing, and that it was for this reason that he just made his lips quiver. So they decided that they could not make him king. Rejecting him, they decided to make the Enlightenment Being the king.

Saying this, the Buddha ended the Jātaka story of Pādañjali.

"The prince Pādañjali at that time is today the monk Lāḷudāyi. And the wise advisor to the king was I who am today the Buddha, the fully enlightened one."

The moral: "Though they may try, fools cannot hide their ignorance."

The Story of Something Comparable to a Kiṁsuka Tree[71]
(Kiṁsukopama-Jātaka)

O nce, when the fully enlightened one was living in Jetavanārāma, he delivered this Jātaka story with regard to the *Kiṁsukopama Sutta*.[72] The circumstances of its delivery are as follows:

Four monks requested meditational subjects from the Buddha. Having learned them, they went to the forest and meditated. One of them meditated on the basis of the six sensual contacts [*cha-phass' āyatana*],[73] and he became an Arahant. Another one became an Arahant by meditating on the five aggregates [*pañcakkhaṇḍha*].[74] The next one attained Arahant-ship by meditating on the four great elements [*catu-mahābhūta*].[75] The last one became an Arahant by meditating on the loathsomeness of the body [*asubhabhāvanā*]. After gaining Arahant-ship, the four went together to see the Buddha. "We four have become Arahants. How did we all reach the same goal from four different types of meditation?" The omnipresent

---

71 The Kiṁsuka tree (*Butea frondosa*), literally, the "what do you call it" tree, has small red flowers that grow in bunches at the ends of its branches, and has a very hard core. Foxes, seeing the small red flowers at the ends of its branches in the moonlight, are deceived into thinking that they are meat and jump up to try to get them.

72 This *sutta* would appear to be the same as the *Kiṁsukā Sutta* of the *Saṁyuttanikāya*.

73 The six sensual contacts, or organs of sense, are the eyes, the ears, the nose, the tongue, the body, and the mind. *Phassa* is the fundamental fact in a sense impression. It consists of a combination of the sense, the object of contact, and the recognition of a feeling.

74 The five aggregates are form, feeling, perception, volitional formation, and consciousness.

75 Earth, water, fire, and air.

one said, "You are like four different brothers who asked about the flower of a Kiṁsuka tree." They asked, "How so?" The Buddha then told them an old story.

At one time, King Brahmadatta was ruling the city of Benares. That king had four sons. Those four one day asked their charioteer, "Can you show us the flower of a Kiṁsuka tree?" He thought, "It is not good to show them the Kiṁsuka tree together." Thinking this, he took one prince by chariot and showed him a dried out, hard cored tree [when buds were just sprouting from the stems]. The second prince was shown the tree with newly sprouted green leaves. The third prince was shown the tree with blossoming flowers. The fourth prince was shown the tree with mature leaves of an amber color that were ready to fall off.

One day, when the princes were talking with one another, the topic of the Kiṁsuka tree arose. One of the brothers said, "It is like a burnt stump." The second one said, "[No], it is like a banyan tree." The third one said, "[No], it is like a tree on which there are hanging pieces of meat." The fourth one said, "It is like all trees of the fall season." The four brothers then began to argue, not being able to agree that they had all seen the same tree. So they went to their father and asked, "Father, what sort of tree is the Kiṁsuka tree? We cannot agree." And the father said, "What did each of you say?" And they told him what each of them had said. Then the father, the king, said, "Children, you have all seen the Kiṁsuka tree, but at different times. As you did not ask the charioteer when he showed you the tree what it was like at other times in the year, and as he did not tell you this, there has arisen in your minds doubt as to the nature of the tree. You must understand that the tree is not the same as you saw it forever. After the fall, it has no leaves and looks like a dried out stump. When leaves are sprouting, it looks like a banyan tree. When it is in bloom, it looks like pieces of meat are hanging from its branches. When the leaves are ready to fall, it looks like a leafy golden-colored Acasia tree [Sinh. Mahari tree]. Therefore, you must understand that the Kiṁsuka tree, while a single thing, appears at different times in different ways. With each season, it changes. But it is the same tree." Saying this, he removed their doubt.

The omnipresent one used this example to explain to the four brother monks the different insights that had been gained by meditating on four different subjects, each leading to Arahant-ship. As they had not gained the stream entrance state of mind first, the Buddha gave them four different meditations each matched to their individual natures. Though using four meditations, it is only one Nibbāna [state of release from re-becoming] that is attained.[76]

Explaining this, the Buddha ended this Jātaka story of something comparable to a Kiṁsuka tree.

"At that time, the King of Benares was I who am today the Buddha."

The moral: "One thing can have many different faces."

---

76   There are according to Buddhist teachings six different types of character. It is for this reason that the four brother monks, none of whom had first entered the stream entrance state of mind, were each given a different meditation though all lead to the same goal. Once an individual attains the stream entrance state of mind, it is usual that meditation on loving kindness [mettā] in the face of anger [paṭigha] is practiced to reach Arahant-ship. The six different types of character are lustful [rāgacarita], hateful [dosacarita], foolish [mohacarita], confident [saddhācarita], intelligent [buddhicarita], and indecisive [vitakkacarita].

The Story of Sālaka[77]
(Sālaka-Jātaka)

When the Buddha who became a Kappadduma tree [Skt. Kalpadruma tree], a tree that lasts throughout the entire aeon, for his Sakyā kin was living in Jetavanārāma, this story was told with regard to a certain elderly monk. The circumstances of its delivery are as follows:

An elderly monk ordained a young man whom he treated very badly. The young novice, unable to tolerate his punishments, became disheartened and disrobed. Then the elderly monk went after him and wanted him to be re-ordained. Trying to persuade him, he said, "Young son, your robes shall be your own. I also have other robes, and I shall give them to you, too. Come with me, and be ordained again." The young man said, "I do not wish to be re-ordained." After the elder monk pleaded again and again, the young man finally decided to become a monk again. From the day that he was re-ordained, the elder monk mistreated him again. And he could not stand the mistreatment. So, for the second time, he disrobed. After that, the elderly monk again asked the young man to be re-ordained. Following him, he tried over and over again to persuade him to be ordained again. But the young man would not. And he went on his way.

The monks who were gathered one evening in the preaching hall were talking about this. They said, "The young man was of a gentle disposition. But the elderly monk had a harsh nature. Because of this misfortune, the young novice lost his monkhood."

While they were talking in this way, the Buddha entered and asked, "Oh monks, what were you talking about before I came here?" The monks

---

77   Literally, Pāli *sālaka* means 'brother-in-law.' 'Brother-in-law' is often used in South Asia as a term of abuse.

told the Buddha about what they were talking. The omnipresent one said, "Oh monks, not only today, but even in the past this young monk left this elderly monk after seeing his cruel nature." The monks then requested the omnipresent one to disclose the old story. And the Buddha then disclosed the ancient story. This is how it was:

At one time, King Brahmadatta was ruling the city of Benares. At that time, the Enlightenment Being was born in a landowner's family. He lived by selling rice.

At the same time, a snake charmer raised a monkey which he trained and to which he gave medicine to swallow that was an antidote to snake bite, so that the monkey could play with the snakes.

Once, at the time of a festival in the city, the snake charmer left his monkey with the rice merchant and went off to have a good time. When he returned, he asked the rice merchant for his monkey. The monkey, hearing the snake charmer's voice, came to him with a happy mind. On seeing him, the snake charmer beat the monkey with a bamboo stick, tethered him with a rope, and took him away with him.

When the man became tired, he tied the monkey to a nearby mango tree and lay down to rest under the tree. When the monkey saw that the man was asleep, he freed himself from the tether and climbed up the mango tree. He ate a mango, and dropped the mango seed on the man. The man woke up and looked up at the monkey. Seeing the monkey up in the tree, he wanted to get him down and thought that he would do so by deceiving the monkey. So he said, "Oh, my dear, you are my only son. Whatever I own, it is all yours, my son. Please come down, Sālaka, from the tree, and come home with me."

The monkey said, "I came to you before on hearing your voice, with loving kindness. And you, seeing me, hit me with anger, using a bamboo stick. So, I will not come with you." Saying this, he scurried away.

The man became very upset. And he went home with sadness.

Saying this, the Buddha ended the story of Sālaka.

"The monkey at that time was this young lad. The snake charmer was this elderly monk. The rice merchant was I who am today the Buddha."

The moral: "Those who treat people with roughness, end up living their life alone."

$$\boxed{250}$$

The Story of a Monkey[78]
(Kapi-Jātaka)

When the omnipresent one who is a raft for crossing the ocean of re-becoming [saṁsāra] was living in Jetavanārāma, he delivered this Jātaka story with regard to a monk who was a hypocrite. These are the circumstances of its delivery:

A certain hypocritical monk who was in the practice of deceiving others was brought before the Buddha. The Buddha said, "Oh monks, not only today, but even in the past this monk tried to deceive others with his hypocritical mind when trying to warm himself by a fire during the rainy season." Then the monks asked the Buddha to disclose the former story. When so requested, the Buddha disclosed the old story as follows:

At one time, King Brahmadatta was ruling the city of Benares. At that time, the Enlightenment Being was born as a householder in Benares. That householder, after his wife passed away, took his children and retired to the forest where he became an ascetic. He also ordained his children as ascetics. While they were in the forest, the rainy season came and it began to rain with torrential downpours.

At this time, a certain monkey got very wet and became tormented by the cold. He saw a fire in the hermitage and thought it would be good if he could get into the hermitage and warm himself by the fire. Thinking this, he disguised himself with some clothes that belonged to a dead ascetic. He thought that if he were to go to the hermitage not dressed like this, they would chase him away. Dressed in this manner, he approached the hermitage as a guest ascetic, standing outside near the hermitage's door holding a walking stick.

---

78 Compare the Makkaṭa-Jātaka [No. 173], which is almost the same.

The Enlightenment Being at that time was lying on a cot and his [eldest] son was massaging his feet. His son saw the monkey who was disguised as an ascetic. Seeing him, and thinking that he was a guest ascetic, he said to his father, "Father, there is a revered ascetic with controlled sensual desires suffering from the cold and waiting patiently outside for us to give him warmth. Would it not be good to invite him into the hermitage and let him warm himself?"

The Enlightenment Being thought that he should see what his son was talking about, and he got off his cot and looked out the door. Immediately, he understood that this was not a true ascetic, but was a monkey. He said to his son, "He is not an ascetic with a restrained mind. He is a monkey! If we take him into the hermitage out of compassion to warm himself by the fire, no doubt he will burn down the hermitage." Saying this, he took a hot firebrand and chased away the monkey. That monkey never again came back to that place.

The Enlightenment Being, developing his meditation in that hermitage, achieved the fivefold miraculous powers and the eightfold concentrations. He taught meditation to his children, and without falling from his attainments, after his death he was born in the Brahma world.

Saying this, the Buddha ended this Jātaka story of a monkey.

"The monkey at that time was this hypocritical monk who tries to deceive people. The ascetic's son was Prince Rāhula. And the ascetic was I who am today the fully enlightened one."

The moral: "Being cunning fools no one but oneself."

ABOUT PARIYATTI

Pariyatti is dedicated to providing affordable access to authentic teachings of the Buddha about the Dhamma theory (*pariyatti*) and practice (*paṭipatti*) of Vipassana meditation. A 501(c)(3) non-profit charitable organization since 2002, Pariyatti is sustained by contributions from individuals who appreciate and want to share the incalculable value of the Dhamma teachings. We invite you to visit www.pariyatti.org to learn about our programs, services, and ways to support publishing and other undertakings.

Pariyatti Publishing Imprints

Vipassana Research Publications (focus on Vipassana as taught by S.N. Goenka in the tradition of Sayagyi U Ba Khin)

BPS Pariyatti Editions (selected titles from the Buddhist Publication Society, copublished by Pariyatti)

MPA Pariyatti Editions (selected titles from the Myanmar Pitaka Association, copublished by Pariyatti)

Pariyatti Digital Editions (audio and video titles, including discourses)

Pariyatti Press (classic titles returned to print and inspirational writing by contemporary authors)

Pariyatti enriches the world by

- disseminating the words of the Buddha,
- providing sustenance for the seeker's journey,
- illuminating the meditator's path.

www.ingramcontent.com/pod-product-compliance
Lightning Source LLC
Chambersburg PA
CBHW051825170626
46807CB00003B/1031